A TWIST OF POWER

BOOK 3 OF THE MADELINE JOURNEYS

P. A. WILSON

FREE EBOOK

Claim your copy of Obstacles of Magic when you use the QR code to sign up for my newsletter and learn more about Madeline's history with magic.

---

*M*adeline held the yellow ribbon and stared at Blu. The little monk was sitting across from her, a matching ribbon laid across his upturned palms. He was muttering so quietly that she had to strain to hear the words he spoke. Her responses to his statements were the only things keeping the spell intact until they finished.

"The net holds against all forces." Blu's voice held no sign of the effort he was pouring into the spell.

"Against all forces, the net flexes to hold," Madeline whispered. She tried to keep her fingers light on the ribbon, because it represented the net of protective spells they held over Arabela's house. If she held the ribbon too tightly, the net would become rigid and, with enough force, shatter rather than flex.

Three days ago, when she'd returned from the Choi temple with her friends, Madeline had hoped that the threats against Arabela's son would fade away. Until her best friend was safe, she wasn't going to return home. Until she returned home, Madeline feared she would never be able to have her own child. The life she'd been living on the road was too stressful. Unfortunately, the threat was still active and growing worse.

It was getting more difficult as time passed to not push back on the attacks. What she really wanted to do was blast all the power back down the line and fry the magic of whoever was on the other end. Blu had considered it when she announced the idea, but quickly said that it wasn't possible.

Madeline watched the golden protective net shudder one more time, and then settle, like Jell-O when it was turned out of a bowl. She breathed out a long shuddering lungful of air and waited until Blu told her to stop feeding power to the spell.

"It is enough for now," Blu said after a moment. "Let us rest and eat. I am afraid that each attack is meant to drain us of power until we are unable to repel even a child's effort."

Madeline stretched and felt the knots in her shoulders relax. She took his ribbon and placed both of them in the small travel chest beside the table. "I was almost convinced that this was a peaceful world – well peaceful enough given the way the Scree behave... and the Choi..." She snorted a laugh. "Where did I get that idea? Since you brought me here, I've spent most of my time fighting off one or another of the species of the world." *And killing too many beings to save the people she loved.* In her old life, she defended people in court not in battle. There no one had died.

Blu stood, only coming up to her shoulder, and took her arm. *He must be shrinking. We used to be closer to the same height. Now he must be only about four feet tall.*

He led her to the door. "Perhaps the months you spent at your home, with your husband were peaceful enough to make you forget that few living beings are satisfied with what they have in life. With dissatisfaction comes conflict."

Madeline pulled open the heavy wooden door to the room. Arabela's home reminded her of Renaissance chateaux in France – solid and safe. The walls warmed with rich, intricate tapestry, and the floors with bright rugs. "Perhaps, but these last few weeks have pushed those memories to the back of my mind."

"Well, we are safe for now," Blu said pulling her toward the stairs. "I smell pastry. Let us join whoever is baking and hope for a taste."

Madeline inhaled the aroma of butter and cinnamon; the intensity made her stomach rumble. Magic took a lot out of her. It also allowed her to eat whatever she wanted. Practicing spells was better than any boot camp program – and usually more fun. "Good idea, and maybe Callisra will be there and we can help to organize the wedding. Anything will be more interesting than casting protection spells." *Who would have guessed I'd become tired of magic?*

Blu started down the staircase. "Indeed; a happy occasion is just what we need to refresh our spirits." He turned toward her, a sly smile on his face. "I am surprised at Simon's hurry to perform the ceremony. He has not shown himself to be comfortable with committing to one woman. Is this normal for men from your world?"

When Madeline was transported to Cartref, Simon came with her. In their old world, he'd been her assistant. When they arrived here, he'd started a rock band within a few days. That band had been the distraction when the attack on Sayer Goddard had happened. Now he was managing the music business for what seemed like the whole world.

Madeline laughed; the last of the weight of the worry she'd been carrying since this morning's attack started lifting from her shoulders. "I suspect you are behind the haste. I thought you won that pool the goblins started. Didn't you pick a date in the next couple of weeks?"

"Perhaps I have counseled him to hasten the date. But no one has won until the wedding takes place." Blu's smile was all innocence, and it made Madeline laugh again.

"I think you're right. With these attacks, it's probably a good idea to get the formalities over with in case...well let's not guess what might happen."

Crossing the great hall with its fireplace and scattered chairs, they entered the kitchen. As they stepped through the archway, a warm blanket of belonging wrapped around Madeline, something she'd never felt back in her world of lawyers, and career momentum, and frozen dinners. The room was large, hot, and full of savory aromas. The chatter of the kitchen staff was a counterpoint to the sound of crackling logs in the ovens.

Simon, dressed in a white tunic over forest green trousers, was charming a tray of cinnamon buns from the cook. Callisra, raven hair pulled into a simple braid, was sitting beside Arabela, their heads bent over a gurgling bundle in Arabela's arms. Tadric, heir to the Summer Lands, and the target of these attacks. The child shared his mother's green eyes, but his curly hair was dark brown.

Madeline left Blu and poured mugs of caf. Before she filled the last one, Jode joined her at the counter. Even after a year, her breath caught when he was near. Tall, blond, and romance-novel handsome, he had captured her heart despite her reservations. "I missed you," he whispered in her ear. "I will be glad to have you to myself again when this threat is over."

"Come and see what my son has learned," Arabela called before Madeline could answer him.

Arabela sat Tadric on the floor and the child remained upright without support. "You see, how strong he is?" She caught him as he started to flop onto his side. "Well, for a short time anyway."

Madeline reached for Tadric and the child held out his arms for her. She settled him on her lap, wondering if her first-born would be a boy.

"You are pale," Jode said as he put a plate of tidbits in front of her. "Are you resting yourself enough? I do not wish to lose you."

She kissed the top of Tadric's head, feeling the tickle of his fine hair against her cheek. Then, smiling up at Jode, she reached for a pastry filled with minced and spiced pork. "We are being careful, maybe too careful. I think we need to talk to Blu again about going on the offensive. If we only repel the attacks as they come, we will eventually fail."

Jode glanced at the boy in Madeline's arms. "The Summer Lands have already lost Alric. If they lose his son, it will leave them open for anyone to take control. There will be bloodshed."

Arabela reached for her son. "If there were other heirs, we would know who was attacking. But Alric was an only child of an only child. And now Tadric is following the tradition."

Madeline took a bite of the pastry before speaking. "Then there must be a way to do something."

"It is too risky to change tactics," Blu said. "If we lose the defense, we lose everything. Neither of us has the power to hold the net alone. Neither of us has the power to attack alone."

Madeline knew her teacher was right, but being right was not going to be good enough if this kept up longer. "There must be a way," she said. "I'm not going to give up so easily."

"YOU CAN SLEEP," Blu said as Madeline jerked out of a doze hours later. "In fact, we should both sleep. No attacks have happened at night yet. I imagine our enemy is as wary of night spells as we are."

Madeline rubbed her eyes to force herself to alertness. She believed Blu but didn't think she would be able to sleep properly knowing she would be woken if... no, when an attack came. "I can nap here. You go to your bed. I'll be able to hold off anything that comes long enough to wake you."

Blu shook his head. "It is not your responsibility alone to keep the wards. But I do not know that I will rest with this threat hanging over us either. Let us talk, perhaps that will soothe us enough to rest."

Madeline felt Blu's touch on the protective net withdraw until it was only a single thread of contact. She followed suit and felt her energy rise slightly with the change. He was right, people here did not do magic at night. She was not sure why. Jode had tried to explain, but she still didn't understand. It didn't matter. Apparently, spells could continue through the night, they just couldn't be cast in safety. So, the net would survive until dawn when they would have to refresh the power.

"Let me get someone to bring us warm tea," she said, rising from the chair to open the door. "It will help us to relax."

A servant was waiting in a chair outside the door. Madeline knew everyone in the household was prepared to support them, but she still felt guilty that this maid was losing her sleep on the off chance they needed something. "Mary, can you bring us some tea. And then you can go to your bed. We won't need anything more tonight."

The girl nodded and slipped away toward the stairs. Madeline returned to the room and moved the throw cushions from the two upholstered chairs so they could curl up. That way, if they fell asleep, at least they would be comfortable. Mary returned with tea and two bowls of oatmeal, rich with cream and dried fruit. "Cook said this will help you sleep."

When they were alone again, Madeline settled into one of the chairs and waited until Blu did the same.

"I think we need a plan." She poked the spoon into the porridge but didn't feel like eating. Her nerves were shredded from just waiting and waiting. "Whoever is attacking isn't going to get bored and just stop."

Blu didn't answer for a few minutes. Only the fact he sipped his tea let Madeline know he was still awake. She knew better than to interrupt his thoughts. Even if she had a plan, he would know something that would improve it. That is if she could convince him to go on the attack.

Finally, he placed his cup on the wide arm of his chair. "You think I am willing to outwait our attacker, but I have been thinking the same thing. We are at a disadvantage. It is taking all of our power to hold the protections, and we will fail if that does not change."

Madeline rose to get the teapot. Topping off both cups, she said, "Is there someone we can trust to help us?" There were no others capable of magic in Arabela's household as far as Madeline knew, and they couldn't spare the energy or time to call someone from far away.

"There is someone. I have not asked him yet, because I thought we would have solved this problem by now."

Attacks on Tadric were more than a problem, but Blu was the master of the understatement, so Madeline didn't argue. "Who? I thought I knew everyone here. Has someone come in the last few days?"

"You forget about the musicians. Zora is an Eldman as well as a talented entertainer." Blu reached for his oatmeal and started picking out the fruit and eating it.

In the silence, Madeline thought about how Zora could help. "As far as I remember, Eldmen can only do small magic. And their spells take a long time because of all the chanting."

Blu nodded and continued to pick out the fruit. Madeline handed him her bowl. "Here, you might as well enjoy mine too. So, are you telling me they have more power than it seems? Or am I missing something?"

"No, they use all of their power. Are you sure you do not want any of the fruit?" Blu's question was polite, but he already had a slice of apple in his fingers.

Madeline shook her head and went back to thinking out the answer. Blu rarely told her what she needed to know, so she'd become used to puzzling it out. "So, that means he can't take my place, or yours." She didn't look at Blu. He knew she needed to talk it through before she came to her conclusion. "Can you use him as a battery?"

"What is that?"

"You store power in one and use it later." Madeline had an

ethical twinge about using someone that way; it didn't seem right. "They give you control over their power."

"An interesting idea." Blu placed the bowl on the floor beside his chair. "I have spells that will allow the caster to channel another's power, but it does not require relinquishing control. I do not know if anyone would be willing, or desperate enough, to agree. And I do not know of a spell that will allow you to store magic for use later."

That would have been too easy. Madeline tried to think a path through the growing fog of exhaustion. "He can do another spell. Yes! He can find us help, or he can seek a clue to the identity of whoever is attacking us."

Blu smiled at her excitement. "I think we can try both. If we sleep, perhaps one of us can spare some power to his spell and allow him to reach as far as the mountains."

Madeline nodded, the thoughts coming quickly. "We should also send the goblins out to find help from other humans, or perhaps from a Fay? They could even go past the mountains. I hope I can eventually find a spell that will remove that restriction."

Blu curled up in his chair. "Another very good idea. Now sleep. I fear we will be tested again in the morning."

Madeline watched her teacher slide quickly into sleep. Her mind was still churning, and she needed to let it slow down. If Zora could call someone, she'd suggest a Fay, because they can see at a distance. Blu was certain that the attacks were coming in from the Northeast. Tomorrow she'd ask Jode to show her what was on the map there, other than just mountains.

Tomorrow they would talk to Zora about helping. And to the goblins. They could move fast, not magic, but it seemed like it sometimes.

She blinked and felt her cup slipping from her hand. Placing it on the floor beside her chair, Madeline pulled her shawl around her and curled up to let sleep take her.

Tomorrow, she thought, it will all work out. Tomorrow, they would save the world.

When Zora joined them the next morning, Madeline let Blu talk. She monitored the protective net while they spoke. It left her able to listen, but most of her concentration stayed with the magic. The little she had left was used to worry about how they would channel the Eldmen magic.

"So, it seems if we do not act to identify this attacker, we will soon be too tired to maintain the safely of the household. We need your help," Blue finished.

Zora nodded and walked to the window, his stocky figure blocking most of the light from the opening. "I can lend you my power for a short time. One of you can try to trace the attacks." He returned to the table. "Also, I can ask Urr to go to the Fay."

As she was about to ask more about borrowing magic, Madeline felt a touch from outside the protections. Not an attack, but a gentle test of the strength. "Blu." She beckoned them over.

Blu reached out with his power and felt the spells. "This is not the same person."

Madeline reached for Zora's hand to bring him into their magic loop. She saw his presence in the net as red streaks against the golden glow. So, power was power. As long as Zora accessed his own magic, she could channel it.

"Strong magic," Zora said. "Take what you need of my power. I will not need my magic anytime soon."

Madeline felt power surge through her connection to the Eldman. The net glowed brightly, then settled back to a glimmer. Zora's magic, now a pale-yellow mist, wove itself around the ribbons of her own. The press from the outside came again, gentle but persistent.

"Is there any way we can reach through to find out who this is without weakening the spell?" The touch was so different from the slamming attack that she couldn't imagine it was a trap. This was like a child tugging at a mother's sleeve for attention. The attacks were as brutal as a battering ram on a screen door.

"It will be difficult," Blu said. "Any breach of the dome will open the way for attack. We will have to be very careful."

Zora shifted toward Madeline and slipped his hand to her shoulder. "I can stay in the link and still leave you with your hands free to work the ribbons with Blu," he whispered. Madeline glanced at him. His eyes were shut, and his lips were moving. Eldmen chanted their magic and Madeline knew that Zora would keep his chant going until they told him to stop, no matter how long it took.

She turned to Blu, leaving only a thread of concentration on the protections. "We could ignore this. Perhaps it is a trap."

Blu simply looked at her until she sighed and admitted, "I don't feel any threat. But it could still be a trap. How can we take a chance?"

Instead of answering, Blu opened his chest of ribbons and started picking through them.

Madeline thought about the possibilities. "If you and Zora were ready to deal with anything that happened, I could reach through and connect with whoever this is."

Blu handed her a green ribbon. "Yes, that is how we do it. But I will be the one to reach through. You are linked to Zora already. I will not allow you to be in such danger."

He handed her several more ribbons. Madeline laid them across her lap. "Are you sure I am capable of pulling you back fast enough?"

"It will all be in the ribbons. If you feel any danger, pull them toward you and I will follow."

Blu interrupted Zora's silent chant to explain what they were doing. The Eldman nodded and moved to sit behind Madeline, placing a hand on each of her shoulders. "You will be able to draw from me as quickly as if it was your own power now. Do not speak to me until you are finished, or it will break my access to the magic."

They settled down and Madeline focused on the net. She saw a golden thread snake toward the center of the spell dome. The questioning pressure tapped again. The thread of Blu's power zipped to the dent and wiggled through the weave of the net. Madeline tightened her grip on the ribbons, ready to yank Blu back.

His probe extended through the mesh and stopped. Madeline waited, feeling Zora's power fill her veins, warm and reassuring.

Suddenly a familiar heat rushed toward the net. Attack! Madeline yanked the ribbons into her lap and winced as the flash of gold scored across her senses. She flooded the net with Zora's power.

The attacker flashed away from the net and left.

"It's done," Madeline said, bringing her focus back to the room.

Zora's hands slipped from her shoulders as he stopped muttering. "That was exhilarating. I have never used so much power at one time." He shook himself and reached for one of the breakfast sandwiches.

Blu was wiping his face with a corner of his robe. He was pale but Madeline thought he looked unhurt.

"Did you learn anything before the attack? Was it a trick? Have some tea." Madeline reached for the pot that was warming on the hearth.

Blu accepted a cup, and then motioned for her to sit. "I am fine, Madeline. Keep calm. I believe we have done some damage to our enemy. But, no, it was not a trick. I was able to make contact, but we were torn apart with the attack." He reached to take a muffin from the tray.

"And?"

"Yes, Blu, stop tormenting us," Zora said around a mouthful of sandwich. "What did you learn?"

11

"I learned that we hurt the attacker. I think we will have some time of peace today at least."

Madeline restrained herself. Blu would string this out as long as he could. It was a good sign. If it was bad news, he would have told them straight out. "That is a relief. I think Zora will have to rest and rebuild his energy. So, was it worth the risk?"

"Our visitor told me that the answer lies in The City, and a stranger who is not a stranger."

"That's not much. Was there anything else?"

"The presence was male; that is all I can tell you."

Madeline reached for her own breakfast as she suppressed the urge to press harder for information. She reminded herself that nothing here was simple. "Where is The City?"

Zora pointed toward the mountains. "North, over the mountains. In the Mariai Lands. Two days, if you go by horse. And not too many of you."

Heat rushed through Madeline's body, and then drained away leaving her feeling dizzy and nauseated. She pushed aside her plate and said, "I think we need to go tomorrow."

Blu nodded as he picked fruit from the muffin. "It will be good to have those attacks come to an end."

The nausea passed, leaving behind a ravenous hunger. She watched the two men as she devoured a muffin; Blu, tiny and deceptively fragile, looking serene as usual; Zora, solid and stern, his movements deliberate as he chose his food from the plate.

"How will we know you are safe?" she asked, hoping for some kind of magical cell phone.

Blu smiled at her, "You must have faith, Madeline. We will endure until we no longer need to." When she opened her mouth to ask for something more concrete, he chuckled. "And I think we will send you a message if anything changes."

2

———

The last time she'd traveled toward the mountains, Madeline had tried her best to keep the group small. A futile effort as their party had grown to almost twenty people in the end. And all of them had proven useful.

This time, only three people accompanied Madeline. Jode who would never have stayed behind, Simon, and Callisra. In the rushed hours of preparation, someone had managed to find a few minutes to hold the wedding ceremony. Simon had promised a celebration party when they returned, but neither wanted to leave on this mission with their vows unsaid.

Now they rode across the rolling grassland to the north of Arabela's home. In the distance, a forest stood between them and the line of mountains on the horizon.

"We will be at the pass by nightfall," Jode said. "The way through is easy; if we do it in the light. In the dark, it can be treacherous, so we will camp before crossing."

They traveled at a fast walk. The horses would go a long way at that pace and still be rested enough for a speedy journey to The City. Madeline tried to imagine what a city – or rather The

City – in Cartref would be like. Probably no skyscrapers like she was used to, maybe she wouldn't call it a city at all.

"Callisra," Madeline called over her shoulder to the couple. "Tell me again what you remember of The City."

"I'm not sure my memories will be useful," she answered. "I was only a child."

Madeline smiled. "At least you have some memory."

Callisra was quiet for a moment. Then she answered in a voice that seemed still stuck in the memory. "So many people. I remember clinging to my father's hand, worried that I would get lost. And the streets were narrow, and it was hot."

"Anything good?" Simon asked.

"It was peaceful. Even with all the people, everyone kept the rule of peace within the walls." Callisra added laughing, "And the food and candy were delicious."

Madeline joined the laughter but wished there was something else she could use to make a plan. She hated going in blind. They only had one contact and that was not even the person who sent the message. The touch of the messenger was torn away before Blu could identify their ally.

"You are quiet, my love," Jode's voice broke through her musing. "Are you fretting about what we might find?"

"You know me too well. I'm not really fretting. It's hard to worry about a plan being successful when you don't have one. All we know is that Blu's friend Zerenia might be able to tell us something about our mystery man."

Callisra nosed her horse between them. "I don't think Blu would have sent us to her otherwise. The Mariai visions usually turn out to be right. The trick is to interpret them correctly."

"Isn't that always the problem?" Simon asked. "Prophecies, visions, messages from beyond… they are all a hundred percent right in hindsight."

Madeline laughed, deciding to enjoy the ride rather than do her usual worrying about controlling the future. "I guess I'm missing the old days when I would take the time to prepare for court. No, not that kind of court," she added at the confused look on Jode's face. "Anyway, why is it called The City? I mean we've seen small towns and villages, but nothing like what I would call a city."

Jode moved his horse off the path so that they could ride together. He increased the pace slightly before answering, "It is the only port on this part of the world. Because of that, it attracts people who wish to travel, or set up business. Ports have a lot of visitors and they need places to stay, goods to buy."

Ports were the same from world to world, Madeline reflected. "How many people live there?"

"Four or five thousand, I expect. No one has counted," Jode answered. "Most are Mariai, but I expect we will find elves, and goblins, and even some Scree. Most beings have some residence or business in The City."

Elves? From what little she'd heard they weren't the Tolkien version – or any of the Tolkien versions to be accurate. Something between a scholar and a berserker was as close as anyone came to describing them.

"Maybe after we find and stop whoever is attacking, we can spend some time exploring The City?" She mentally crossed her fingers that it would be that simple. She was getting tired of rushing around the countryside rescuing people. It felt like forever since she'd been in her own home, not just two weeks. A few days to deal with this problem and maybe she could go home to the Lower Plains.

"I imagine we will see most of it in our search for the culprit," Jode said. "But it would be pleasant to have time with my wife with nothing to do but explore and…" He grinned at her in a way that made her blush.

Callisra giggled. "It is nice to know that, even after almost a year, you can behave like newlyweds."

.   .   .

HOURS LATER, Madeline was getting tired of the sameness of the grasslands. The rolling landscape lulled her mind and she shook her head again to wake herself up. There was enough breeze to move the grass in gentle waves, which added to the soporific effect.

The edge of the forest beckoned with the promise of coolness and variety of scenery. The sun was not so hot it burned, but it was hot enough to drain her energy. They rode more or less side by side, but from what she could see of the path through the trees, they would have a road to travel soon. Perhaps they would be able to move faster on firmer ground.

She kneed Thunder to a trot and said, "Let's pick up some speed. If I'm going to fall asleep, I'd rather do it when I have my bedroll beneath me."

Looking back, she saw the grin on Jode's face as he urged Ice Storm to race her. Simon and Callisra laughed and joined the scramble for the tree line.

"Last one there is a rotten—" her challenge died on her lips as an arrow slapped into the ground ahead of her. She turned to see who had shot it.

"Madeline, get down and find cover," Jode's voice cut through her confusion.

She spurred Thunder to a gallop and glanced around to see Simon join Jode in scanning the grassland behind them as their horses raced forward. Callisra matched Madeline's pace as they crossed into the shaded canopy of the forest onto a well-packed dirt road just ahead of their husbands.

"Into the trees," Jode shouted.

Madeline kneed her horse and veered off the road praying that Simon and Callisra would split up. Whoever was behind that arrow would be taking aim again, and if they could present more targets, they could make it harder to do too much damage. And, perhaps, find way to figure out who was attacking.

A few feet into the forest there was enough cover, so Madeline pulled on the reins. She could hear brush snapping and swishing off to her right, one of the others in her party barreling along to safety. There were no sounds coming from behind.

She brought her horse to a halt and turned him in a space between two giant trees. Jode wouldn't like it, but she had to investigate. Not so long ago, they were attacked when they ascended Severed Pass. That time, it was with a sawed through axle and this time an arrow. Two very different approaches. She hoped that didn't mean more than one person was out to kill one of them.

She slid off the horse and looped the reins over a branch. Then she started back to the road on foot, taking care to put her lessons in tracking to good use. Slipping from tree to tree, Madeline backtracked. There was still no sound coming from behind where they had left the road. Madeline glanced at the trees, wondering if someone was approaching through the tight canopy. No flicker of movement caught her eye. The noise of the horses would have frightened away the birds. Crouching low, she approached the packed earth of the road, stopping only when a low bush covered her.

No one was standing there arrows in hand searching for victims. Madeline slowed her breathing and sent her senses down the road. There were the small touches of animals, but nothing that was big enough to draw a bow. The animals were calm, which indicated whoever had shot the arrow was gone.

Turning her attention around her, Madeline checked to make sure that the attackers hadn't passed them in the rush to escape. The golden glow she knew to be her husband was the only sign of anything larger than a rabbit in the woods. Jode was behind her, and she would have to face his disapproval before they continued to the pass. Before turning to greet him, she sent her senses quickly out ahead, only Simon and Callisra, and it looked like they were back on the road and headed for the pass. Darn! If they had doubled back, maybe she could have deflected the lecture.

"They are gone," Jode said when she met him at the tree where her horse stood placidly waiting to be released. "Our attackers have retreated."

"How did you get there so quickly?" Madeline reached up and tossed the end of the reins over the branch to release her horse. "And how do you know they haven't moved ahead?"

Jode mounted and waited for Madeline to do the same. Then he led her to the road at an angle. When they were trotting toward the pass, he finally answered, "I turned back as soon as I had cover. Ice Storm is trained to move quietly through the woods. When we hunt, I do not always wish to be on foot as I come to my prey."

Madeline wondered if it would be worth investing time to train her horse to do the same but dismissed the idea. She didn't want to take part in the hunt and hoped to eventually live a quiet life. "I know the attackers are gone, but how do you know they aren't running ahead to set a trap."

Jode turned to look at her and Madeline sensed the lecture on her behavior was about to start. Jode never yelled at her, but his disappointment hurt. Although not enough for her to be a meek obedient wife. Fortunately that wasn't what Jode wanted, and he was smart enough to know it. "If we had time, I would take you back and teach you the finer points of tracking. I saw evidence that only one person was on the attack. Others came, and the tracks lead back to the grasslands. It is no guarantee that we will not be troubled again, but we have some time to travel in peace."

"It's like the wagon axle." Madeline urged her horse into a faster gait. Short bursts of speed would not harm the animal. "An attack with no follow up."

"I am confused as to the approach as well." Jode glanced behind as he spoke. "I have not heard of this type of attack. I wonder if it is simply uncoordinated, or if they are attempting to frighten us until they finally close in."

Madeline considered what she knew about terrorism, and guerrilla fighting, neither seemed to fit this situation. "If we are safe for now, let's catch up to the newlyweds and get to the pass."

Jode kept his eyes on the path ahead. "Now, perhaps, we can talk about your risky behavior."

Madeline saw that the trees were thinning out ahead. "Are we almost out of the forest?"

"No, but there are clearings. We will stop in one for a rest soon." He glanced at her. "If you are killed, we will not be successful on this task. I do not think we will be able to solve this without magic, and you are the only one in our party with anything other than healing talent. Will you allow me to protect you?"

She wanted to say yes. She knew it would be impossible for her to stick to that agreement. Before she could answer, Jode continued, "No. That is not a fair request. Will you at least allow me to help?"

A bird called from a bush to the side of them, its mate replied from a neighboring shrub. "Yes. I promise. If there is time, I will always ask you to help me."

"Always. Regardless of how much time is available, Madeline." Jode pulled closer. "Promise me that you will not leave me behind to avoid asking."

Madeline stared into his eyes, the blue darkened with worry. "I promise."

FOUR HOURS LATER, the forest was thinning, and Madeline hoped they were close to the pass where they would stop for the night. Her muscles felt like she had been in the saddle for days, sore and bruised.

Other than the aborted attack earlier, nothing had happened

to break the monotony of the ride. Conversation had dried up after the last stop where the horses had rested, and the humans had walked off the stiffness.

"Tell me about this pass," Madeline said, hoping to restart some discussion – if only to move time along. It already felt like she was taking too long to stop the attacks.

They were riding two abreast, Madeline and Callisra behind the two men. Jode turned to look at them and said, "I have been told that the pass is more like a break in the foothills. The mountain range is almost at its end this far east. I only have second-hand information. Callisra, how did you travel when you came here?"

"As I said, I was just child. We came in a wagon," she said. "We did go over the pass in the morning, but that is all I remember. But I'm not sure we came this way. Is the pass wide enough for a wagon?"

"Barely," Jode said. "It is unusual for wagons to travel any other way but along the coast. A small pass farther that way." He pointed to the right.

Madeline waited but no one said anything more. The buzz of insects the only sound that accompanied their horses' dull clump on the packed earth. Finally, she asked, "Why can't we go over before morning? I can cast light, if that's the problem."

Simon groaned. "Are you serious? My bones were looking forward to the rest before we went on."

"Wouldn't you rather get to a real bed faster?" Madeline knew that the morning would bring different pains, and she knew that Simon knew that too. She really just wanted to keep talking to push away the anxiety that had ridden with her since the attack. "Isn't it only a few hours from the pass to the entrance to The City? If we could get through when we arrive, we could be eating a real breakfast after a night in a real bed instead of jerky and grains."

The road widened and the men nudged their horses to the side so Madeline and Callisra could ride with them.

Madeline watched Jode. He had on his thinking face. He knew that if he chose the wrong words, she would continue to argue, or perhaps he was used to her arguing for the sake of it. She smiled. It had only been a year and she felt like they knew each other as if they were an old married couple.

He finally said, "In the daylight, we can cross the pass in an hour or so. Your magical light casts odd shadows, which will slow us down and make us jumpy. The City is, indeed, only two hour's hard ride. I do not want to travel at night in an unknown place. If we are attacked again, I want to be able to see what is coming."

Madeline gave up on her halfhearted pressure to move on. Jode was right, unknown terrain was hazardous enough without potential attacks. She was about to voice her capitulation, when her heart stopped beating at the sound of flapping and a loud squawk as a group of birds broke through the underbrush behind them. Jode and Madeline turned their horses and drew weapons before realizing it was only birds.

"Well, that woke me up," Madeline said, sliding her throwing knife back into the sheath on her thigh. "It has been too quiet up to now."

Simon looked at Jode and said, "I think you were right."

"About what?" Madeline looked between Simon and Jode. "Right about what?"

"Have you noticed how quiet it's been?" Simon asked.

Callisra answered, "I just thought it was because the animals are nocturnal."

"Keep moving." Jode shook the reins and his horse stepped forward. "We are being followed."

Madeline flicked a glance around but didn't see anyone. As her horse started after the others, she sent out her senses. Something tickled at the very edge of her reach. How had she missed the clues? Whoever was following was too far behind for her to get more than an impression of anger, hatred, and something else. Far enough behind that she couldn't tell how many, or what kind of being.

"How much farther?" she asked, moving a little closer to the other three.

"To the pass?" Jode asked

"Or at least out of the forest."

Jode looked up as though he could see the sun. Madeline followed his gaze and saw that the canopy had thinned enough to allow them to see where the sun was, low and behind them. The afternoon was slipping away.

"At this speed, we will be out of the trees in a half hour. Then there are several miles of rolling lands before we reach the camp." He glanced back. "When we are out of the forest, it will be difficult for them to follow without being seen."

Madeline nodded and urged Thunder to a faster gait. "Then let's not give them the advantage any longer than we have to."

MADELINE COULD FEEL EYES – or arrows – aiming at her back. "The horses can take a lot more speed, right?" She knew that if push came to shove, the horses were expendable. No matter how much she loved Thunder, if anyone in her party was in danger of being killed, the horses would come in second to the humans. "If we hurry to the pass, I can hide us under a protective spell like I did before, on Severed Pass." *Where it had saved everyone.*

No one took the trouble to answer; they all urged their horses to a trot, then a gallop.

They emerged from the last line of trees and Jode signaled for them to slow back to a trot. "The horses cannot continue at a gallop and still bring us to the pass. We do not want to walk from the pass to The City."

Madeline reluctantly obeyed; the itch of eyes on her back

almost overwhelming. Even at their slower pace, the trees faded into a green line behind them in only a few minutes. All of them rode side by side in grass that was up to the withers of the horses. Looking back, Madeline saw the grass ripple just at the edge of her sight.

"Someone is following, and they are closer than they were," she said, keeping her voice low. "Not a lot of people."

Jode didn't turn. "I saw them exit the forest. I should say I saw the effect of them leaving. I do not know who it is."

She glanced back again. "They are falling behind now. On foot, not that fast. Any clues?"

Simon drew closer. "Can't you use some magic to see them or something?"

"Not and stay on my horse. We just need to keep going and hope we can gain enough lead to set our spell tonight."

The ground started to rise, and Madeline saw that what she had taken for low-lying clouds was the foothills they had to cross.

Callisra rode ahead to the top and waited for them to catch up. When they gathered, Jode staring back the way they had come, Callisra said, "The hills are not an easy ride. Look, there's a path, but there is very little cover."

Madeline surveyed the road as far as she could see. A track wide enough for two horses, a broad shoulder on one side, and a rock face on the other. This path had been cut out of the rock. If it continued this way, they could go fast enough to gain more time on their pursuers. If it didn't stay this way, maybe she could cast the spell, and they could travel slowly. No, even if it got rougher, they needed to travel fast. "There will be no point in casting a concealment if our pursuers are able to see me do it. We need to get as far ahead as possible before stopping."

Jode turned his horse to face them. "They are perhaps a half hour behind us. Is there anything we can do to protect ourselves, or the horses, for this?"

"Yes, can you do that invisible spell again, like when we rescued Lee?" Simon automatically took over the job of watching their trail as he spoke.

Madeline sighed. They seemed to think she could solve everything with magic. "It doesn't work that way. I could cast it, but it would be too easy for someone to wander too far out of the spell. Any dust we raised would become visible. The spell isn't meant for this kind of situation." She glanced again, not seeing any movement. "We need to just go, but we have a few minutes. Callisra, can you check to see if any of the horses are hurt?"

She nodded and dismounted to start running her hands over the legs of the mounts.

Madeline glanced behind them. "I'll try to see what is happening behind us while we wait."

She slipped into a trance and threw her senses toward the grasslands. At first, she couldn't quite cast far enough. Her power resisted her commands, as if it had a plan, as if it were sentient. Then it flowed as easily as usual. She felt the distance in her mind, a mile or two back, something was there. But it was a void, and it was moving. She probed gently at what felt like a bubble, to no avail. Taking a quick assessment of the size of the bubble, she drew her consciousness back to the group. "No luck. They have something that bars my magic from details. From the size of the blankness, it's probably a party of four or five people." *At least it's not an army.*

"No injuries," Callisra reported.

"Then we go," Jode said. "Simon, take the lead. I will guard the rear. Madeline and Callisra, stay between us."

They started forward at a working trot. As fast as the horses could go and maintain the gait for long enough to make a difference.

The sun was setting as they pulled up for a rest at the entrance to the pass. "Do you have any idea where they are?" she asked as Jode joined them. "Do we have time for a quick rest?"

He rose in his seat and scanned the area before answering. "I lost sight of them. It could be that they have given up, or –"

"Or, they have found a way to catch up," Madeline finished his statement. "Let me check."

Not waiting for agreement, Madeline sent her power out in a circle as far as she could reach. This time her power answered immediately. She sensed nothing more than a few field animals, and what felt like a ten-foot snake. She rolled her shoulders to take the creepiness of the snake essence out of her mind. She pushed out another wave of power, now reaching for the sense of some other magic; still nothing.

"I think we're safe for now, but I don't want to chance it much longer." She returned her gaze to the road ahead. "If we had light, would it make a difference?" Her question was barely audible, she was thinking out loud more than making a plan, so Simon's voice startled her.

"I think we should try," he said. "Light or not, staying here feels like a really stupid idea."

Madeline laughed at the image that came to her mind. "Like a teen slasher movie? The power is out, and the bimbo goes into the basement."

Jode and Callisra gave her the look she was getting used to. It said, '*I don't know what you mean, but please don't try to explain*'.

Simon dismounted before saying, "Yeah. I'm having a difficult time finding it funny though." He grinned and Madeline realized he wasn't taking a jab at her. He continued, "I need to walk for a while, or I might never recover from the saddle."

"I can heal you," Callisra dismounted to stand beside him.

Simon shook his head. "The horses need the rest as much as I do, and you must be as saddle weary as I am. If we walk for a bit, it won't make that much difference. Besides we can eat and drink on the road to make up the time."

Jode also dismounted and held his hand to assist Madeline. "I hear water. The horses need that more than rest. We can stop long enough for the horses and humans to eat and drink, but I think we should be in the saddle as we travel the pass."

Madeline felt her muscles seize up as she tried to walk. Grimacing in pain, she continued, one step at a time, as Jode led them to the river.

A HALF HOUR LATER, Madeline cast the glow spell in front of the horse so that she could lead them through the pass. Jode kept to the rear, alert for the mystery attackers. All of them rode with reins in one hand and the other holding a weapon. Madeline's nerves were vibrating at every skitter of falling pebbles and swoop of night bird. It took all of her concentration to keep the light steady.

Despite the urgency, Jode worried about the horses, so he made them go at a walk to minimize the risk of an injury. The path inclined steadily but the surface deteriorated into ruts and loose rubble. Madeline had to keep reminding herself to breathe. The glow of her spell cast harsh shadows on the walls that rose on either side of them. More than once she raised her throwing knife only to realize it was a shadow of a horse not an attacker.

"If this goes on much longer, I'm going to explode," she said.

A chuckle came from behind her. Callisra was clearly not as wound up. "Madeline, it is not that dire, you can relax a little. There are four of us here. You are not the only one responsible for our safety."

The words caused her to turn in the saddle to see the rest of her party. They followed, arms relaxed, almost lounging on their horses. "Maybe if someone had mentioned that earlier ..." then the tension flowed out and she snorted a laugh at herself. "I guess I was taking the lead a little too seriously. It's not often I'm up here in the front."

It took two hours of careful stepping to get through the pass. As they exited, Madeline's spell spread out to show the terrain ahead. Golden sand dunes rose on each side of a path that curved out of sight.

She moved her horse to the side as the others made it through the narrow opening. As she waited, she sent the light out as far as she could. Nothing changed. Still only sand carved into patterns by the wind.

The sight was enough to take her mind off the immediate danger. "If The City is the only port, how do they send goods to the rest of the land?"

"They go the long way around," Callisra answered. "The wagons don't cross here. Either they travel along the coast and cross through Ale's pass, or they travel the other way and cross at the Narrows pass. I think we must have come through Narrows pass when I came with my parents."

Madeline nodded and looked across the sand. "Can we rely on this path? Does it lead all the way to The City?"

Jode dismounted and tested the sand with his feet. "Yes. But we will have to wait for light to be sure we don't wander off into the dunes."

Simon twisted to look through the gap they had just passed. "Could someone come through a different way?"

"No. The other crossings are at least a day away. And you saw how steep the sides were. No one can come over the mountains. Only one person at a time can come through, so I think we can safely rest here. I will take the first turn at guard."

Madeline couldn't shake the feeling that they were in danger. "I think we should try to leave. I know it will be hard, but even if we go slowly it will get us away from whoever is following us."

Jode wrapped an arm around her and kissed her forehead. "If you can sense the danger, we should go, but I worry that we are tired and that means we may make mistakes. If we rest for a few hours, it will mean a safer passage."

His embrace chased the fears to the edge of her consciousness. "A couple of hours' rest is fine."

.   .   .

MADELINE SHOOK SIMON AWAKE. "It's time. We'll be in The City by morning, even if we travel slowly. Wake the others while I get the horses fed and saddled."

It had only been a couple of hours, but she felt encouraged that no one attacked. Even such a short shift at watch had been difficult for Madeline. Staying alert in such silence after a long day in the saddle was a skill she didn't possess. Her leg would be black and blue from the number of times she'd pinched herself to stop falling asleep. The thought of a bath, and a meal of something other than trail food, almost drowned out the fear that they would be too late. That the attacks on Arabela's home had succeeded.

As she saddled the horses, the others joined her, passing a snack of dried meat, dried fruit, and the last of the water. "What about the horses?" she asked before biting into a dried fig.

"I watered them before I woke you for your shift," Callisra said. "They will be fine as long as we do not push them too hard."

Madeline looked at the sand just beyond the packed earth of their camp. Nothing but dunes curving away, backs shaped by the wind. Everything was a gradient of shadow arranged around a darker line. "Is that the trail?"

Jode nodded. "I am told it will widen as we leave the shadow of the mountains."

Madeline hoped that was soon. Going single file made it too easy to pick them off if an attack came.

"We should travel quickly," Jode said. "I will lead today, perhaps that will save my wife's nerves."

"Thank you," Madeline said without a trace of the sarcasm she would have used at any other time. "I'll take the rear. Throwing knives will do a better job at keeping attackers off us, so we won't have to use our close weapons."

When they mounted, Jode started for the thread of trail.

"Trust your horses. They will not step off the track unless you make them."

HOURS LATER, Madeline wished they had kept a few sips of water in the canteens. She swallowed against the thirst that was threatening to overwhelm her and sent her power out to seek again. Still no presences. The sun was barely over the horizon and she found herself imagining waterfalls and cool baths. No one should travel in this abominable heat.

"Is that The City?" Callisra's voice broke through Madeline's doze.

Looking up she saw a line in the distance, the gold of the sand fading into a darker red.

"It must be," Jode answered. "It is still a long way, but it is nice to see evidence that our journey will eventually be over."

Madeline squinted into the distance, feeling the buzz of faint thoughts along the power thread she'd thrown toward their destination. "Yes, there are people there, lots of them." Hope for shade and water made her almost faint. "Jode is right. It is much farther than it looks. I think, maybe, a couple more hours." How was it possible that this was only two hours of hard riding normally?

Simon's groan sufficed for all of them. Then he cheered a little. "I'm with Jode. At least we know we are going to make it. I've been thinking this track might be going in circles. It's a wonder anyone travels this way."

"Most don't," Jode answered. "And those who use the pass travel at night, crossing the pass in late afternoon and then resting. But they are not worried about pursuit. I did not expect us to travel so slowly and now we are too worn down by the heat to move faster. Perhaps we should have risked injury when it was still dark and cool."

"And perhaps we would be walking now if we had. Don't

second guess yourself, my love." Not having the energy to add anything else, Madeline returned to her half doze. Perhaps when they got closer, they could go faster.

IT TOOK ALMOST four hours for them to approach close enough to see more than just shapes. Jode pointed to the gate. "I was expecting to approach from an angle. It would make sense for protecting The City, but the trail goes directly to the gate." He leaned forward in the saddle. "Look, is that really a fountain I see?"

Madeline started to ask if they could speed up their pace without killing the horses, but as she opened her mouth, Simon fell from his mount.

She reined her horse and leapt to the ground. As she reached to see how badly he was hurt, something whined past her ear.

"Stay down," Jode called, spinning his horse to find the attacker. "Is he harmed?"

Callisra joined Madeline beside Simon, pulling their horses around to form a shield. "No, he will be fine. It is just a bruise."

Madeline glanced up at her husband. "Jode, don't make yourself a target. Ouch." A sharp splinter of stone deflected off Simon's saddle, clipping her ear as it passed. She spun around. "Where are they? Who are they?"

Another stone landed in a puff of dust a foot from where they crouched.

"I cannot see who they are," Jode said as he slipped from his horse. "They are off to the north, but there is magic concealing them. Madeline, can you find them?"

"Forget spending energy to find them. They aren't between us and the gate," Simon said, pulling himself up from the ground. "We can run for it, before they get closer, or cut us off."

Madeline didn't feel good about mounting again and presenting a clear target. "Will the horses make it?"

"Just," Callisra said, running a hand across each mount's flank. "And they will have time to recover fully while we search The City."

"Mount low in the saddle and don't worry about anything but clearing the gate," Jode said. "No matter who they are, they will not risk breaking the peace of The City."

"Okay, together then." Madeline grabbed the pommel of Thunder's saddle and mounted, then dropped low just as an arrow screamed past. The stones were bad enough, but arrows tended to do more damage than a shard of flint.

Jode slapped her horse's rump and the beast took off at a gallop for the gates. Madeline clung to the saddle and listened for other arrows, and other horses. The only hoof beats she could hear were her friends' and they were just behind her. As they sped to the safety of The City, arrows started to stab into the sand to either side of them.

"Are they bad shots, or are we being driven somewhere?" she muttered. Looking ahead, she saw a clear run to the gates, only a hundred feet away. Then an arrow thocked as it pierced the saddlebag, an inch from her leg. Anger flared and she tore the shaft out, holding it in her fist as she crossed through the carved stone gates of The City. Safe.

She reined her horse and spun to watch the others come through. Callisra came first, Simon right behind leaning to cover his wife's back. Jode rode still farther behind, as though he had delayed on purpose.

Madeline's grip on the arrow tightened until she heard a snap as the shaft broke. She could see that the attack was still going on, as Jode raced for the safety of the shade beyond the gates. Arrows followed him, falling to the sand as his horse's rear hooves lifted. Too close.

His horse's head entered The City. He was clear. She started to yell in victory. Then one final arrow found its mark in Jode's shoulder. He slumped in the saddle as Ice Storm took the final steps into the shade.

The world shrank to the shaft of light in the gate. Sounds dropped away to only the beat of Thunder's hooves as Madeline kneed her horse forward. She rode past Jode, instinct holding her in the saddle, knowing that Callisra would make sure he was taken care of.

Thunder managed a gallop all the way back into the sun toward the attackers. Voices called her name, but they sounded miles away. All she saw was a red haze flowing around her like a veil.

Without conscious effort, she sent her magic shooting out on her fury. Seeking revenge on whoever had let that arrow fly.

She heard screaming, and forced her magic farther seeking blood. But nothing was there.

Then someone grabbed her from her saddle and carried her back to The City. Voices came through the screaming, but she couldn't make out any words.

Then someone was shaking her.

"Madeline," Simon's voice cut through the haze. "Stop it. He's going to be okay. Stop screaming."

$\mathcal{M}$adeline came back to her senses slowly, keeping her eyes on the ground until it stopped spinning. Was everyone watching? Were the local authorities on the way? She glanced around and most people were just going about their business. A few looked at her as if worried she might kick off again. Was it because she went mad outside The City? Her symptoms faded slowly. It was the same as the time she'd killed that Scree woman. A threat to Jode had woken some berserker in her. She rested on the edge of the fountain, sipping water to soothe her throat. The red mist still lingered at the very edge of her vision.

The water helped and the world gradually returned to normal; the mist fading to nothing. As she got her equilibrium, the sounds of The City started to filter through the shock of what happened. The trickle of the fountain, the chatter of voices speaking in multiple languages, all combined to bring her that familiar buzz of a city. Not quite as loud as Vancouver, but still oddly comforting.

She turned to look for Callisra, to ask about Jode. She was kneeling beside him, her eyes closed, hands on his chest. Madeline noticed there were only a few bloodstains, and they were not growing. He would survive. The remaining chill of fear was replaced with the heat of The City. She trailed her fingers in the water feeling the coolness as a relief.

Callisra lifted her hands from Jode and said, "You might find yourself sore for a few days, but the wound was not deep."

Simon returned to the square surrounding the fountain as Madeline started to rise. "The horses are stabled. We can get them when we need to." He held up a key on a long chain. "It seems we are trusted to come and go as we please."

On her feet and feeling steady, Madeline looked around her. The square let out onto six narrow streets. The houses were mostly three floors and the top one seemed to lean over just a little, making the street more an open tunnel of deep reds and dull ocher. The walls of the houses looked thick and there were only a few narrow windows facing the square. The place was designed to deal with the heat. She hoped their inn would be cooler for the thick walls.

She watched the bustle around the square. People of all different types. Humans and what must be Mariai by the sheer number of them. They were dressed in loose fitting sleeveless clothes. The Mariai were leanly muscled, like swimmers or long-distance runners. Arms and legs were darkly tanned, but what took Madeline's attention was their faces. Each one, young or old, was tattooed with intricate markings; slashes and dots and stars covered cheeks and brows.

She lifted her eyes from the crowd and focused on Jode. "Any ideas where we start?"

He stood and rolled his injured shoulder before speaking. "Blu seemed to think she lived near the port itself. Perhaps we should just pick a street and follow it to the water?"

Simon handed Madeline her saddlebags. "No need to do that. I asked at the stable and they suggested we go down there." He pointed to a street that ran beside a store displaying cooking pans. "Apparently, she runs a great inn. They send travelers to her all the time."

Madeline hoisted the bag onto her shoulder. "Let's hope her inn has some vacancies." As they walked, Madeline tried not to gawp at the sights, after all she had seen a city before. But this one felt alien and crowded after so long in the country.

There were familiar beings on the streets, humans and Eldmen. But there were some she had never seen before. She leaned in and whispered to Jode, "Those two men, the short ones, are they elves?"

He glanced where she indicated and squeezed her arm. "Yes, they are."

"I expected something different," she said. "I don't know. In my old world, there were so many different ideas of what elves would look like. I just didn't expect them to look so much like humans. Are they all so small and delicate?"

"Yes, those two are typical. Madeline, do not be fooled by their appearance. Elves are fierce and will not stop fighting until the enemy is dead, or the elves are."

Two Scree crossed the street in front of her. "I don't understand how the Scree can be wandering so openly here. They aren't exactly civilized." *More like rampaging Vikings.*

"That's true, but they need supplies. The chalk they use for spell casting is from an island far to the south. This is the place to come for trade, and like everyone else, as long as they stay peaceful inside the walls, they are welcome."

"It still makes me feel like I've got an arrow aimed at my back." Madeline watched the Scree until they entered a small doorway.

Jode slowed and pointed to a sign at the cross street ahead. "I think we have found our inn."

The sign read *The Shallow Tide*. The building looked clean, and the street outside the door was swept. Madeline looked up the face of the inn. Four sets of windows, half with their shutters closed, looked back. A breeze cooled her face and brought the tang of the sea with it.

The four of them went through the open door to a hall where a woman sat at a table. She was older than most of the people Madeline had seen on the streets, the age showing on her face, not in her upright posture or the bright intelligence in her eyes. Her facial tattoos were fading, with only a red star centered on her forehead looking fresh.

She put down a pipe as they approached. "Welcome to my home. How many rooms would you like?" Her voice was deep and rich.

Madeline stepped forward. "Two rooms. We are not sure for how long. We are looking for Zerenia Alewife."

"Yes," the woman said as she reached into a pocket to draw out two keys. "You have come from Blu."

Madeline looked back at the others, no one offered a comment. Turning back to the woman she asked, "How did you know?"

The woman smiled. "I am Zerenia. I know such things."

"Really?" Madeline was torn between amazement at the strength of the power that suddenly radiated like the noon sun, and relief that they didn't have to search any longer. The attack at the gate, after everything that had happened yesterday, had sucked her energy and she was just about ready to sink to the floor and sleep.

Zerenia raised an eyebrow and then suddenly her face softened. "No, I am powerful, but not omniscient. I received a message that Blu was sending someone. I have been expecting you."

The person who sent the warning? "Who sent you the message?" Madeline asked.

"I did not think to ask," Zerenia said. "It does not matter. It was good news, yes? Come. Let me show you to your rooms." She refused to say anything else until they were settled. Zerenia led them to a pair of rooms on the ground floor in the back of the building, and then told them she would meet them over lunch.

It was cool and it was quiet. Madeline dropped the saddlebags on the floor and flopped onto the bed. "I guess we have to let her call the shots."

Jode sat beside her and took her hand. "I think she is giving you a chance to rest. Perhaps to prepare yourself for whatever she has to tell you."

"I guess we have at least an hour before lunch," she said, rolling across the bed toward him. "Not enough time for a sleep, but plenty of time to try out that bathtub."

AN HOUR LATER, Madeline knocked on the room next door. Callisra opened it and whispered, "Simon is sleeping. I don't want to wake him unless you think it necessary."

Madeline shook her head. "I left Jode in dreamland too. He needs to heal. Come on, we'll have a girl's lunch and we can tell them what we learn. I'm sure we can bring them something to eat afterward."

They found Zerenia in a small room to the side of the entrance. She beckoned them to sit at the table, which was covered in small plates of delicious smelling food.

"Eat a little first," Zerenia said. "I know you must be curious, but I must prepare for the answers."

Callisra handed Madeline a plate and started filling her own with morsels of what smelled like mushroom balls. "Prepare yourself?" she asked. "Can't you just tell us what you know?"

Madeline tasted a white nut that had been rolled in spices. "This is delicious," she said, waiting for the answer to Callisra's question.

Zerenia passed a cup of cool liquid. "Ah, thank you. My cook has a way with spices does he not? To answer your question, I do not yet know anything. I have been given the knowledge that I

37

can help, but I cannot perform the magic until I have you here. I think you will have the energy to find this help now that you have taken the edge off your hunger." Clearing a space on the table, Zerenia took Madeline's hands in hers. "Healer, please be ready to act if this takes too much out of either of us."

Madeline had no time to worry about what could be taking too much out of them. As soon as Zerenia's eyes closed, Madeline felt a tug at her power. Zerenia sighed and the tug released. "I see two men," Zerenia said. "Both are capable of great good and great damage. One is not your friend, the other may be."

Madeline waited for more, hoped for more. When Zerenia was clearly not going to say anything, Madeline asked, "Is there a way to know which man is attacking the Summer Lands?"

Zerenia squeezed Madeline's fingers and that tug at her power came back for a fraction of a second. Blowing through tight lips, Zerenia let go of Madeline's hands and sat back. "No. I cannot describe either man. Even if I could, it is impossible to see which is doing this harm. I only know that you will find an unlikely ally somewhere. And something more that is too far away for me to see."

Madeline realized she'd been hoping for something more direct and should have realized nothing that involved magic would ever be direct. Still, an address was probably too much to expect, but a hint at an identity would have helped.

"Do not look so disappointed, Madeline," Zerenia said. "I have seen that you will meet one man today. Be aware of missiles from above."

Madeline wanted to go searching as soon as Zerenia was finished, but her body was not cooperating. Pains and stiffness fought her worry about Arabela and Tadric and won. She needed to give her body some time to heal from the saddle.

. . .

38

THREE HOURS LATER, Madeline sat in the lobby waiting for the others to join her.

"How shall we proceed?" Callisra asked as she led Simon into the lobby. "If we split up, we can cover so much more of The City."

"Yes, but we could waste time reporting in." Madeline looked down the hall to their door. "When Jode gets here, I think we should go together to the docks and spend as much time as we can searching that area. We have to figure out the neighborhoods as well as who this person is." She jumped up, her impatience forcing her into action. "I'll be back in a second, I don't know what's keeping Jode." She started down the hall, worried that Jode had been more injured than they thought.

Before she got more than a few steps into the dimness, she heard Jode call her from the street. Turning she saw him silhouetted in the doorway and her breath caught. Even as a shadowy outline, he was beautiful. She turned back to the entrance and felt the heat of the day beat on her as she approached the door.

"I didn't want to take the chance we would get lost, so I thought a little reconnaissance might be in order. I've been talking to the bookseller across the street," Jode said, nodding his head toward the curtained door of the shop directly across from the inn. "He gave me the lay of the city."

"And?" Madeline pushed aside the twinge of annoyance. It was not important that she make all the decisions. "Did you get any useful advice?"

Jode nodded. "Yes. He suggested that the docks would be full of gossip. It is a good place to find information if you are careful not to seem nosy."

Madeline stepped out into a street that was much different from what they had walked through early this morning. Now people moved with clear purpose. Most heading toward where she knew the port was located from Zerenia's directions. Others hurried in the opposite direction, hefting baskets of fish, or rolls of fabric in bright colors. There were carts lining the street farther down. Calls of 'fresh bread', 'ripe plums picked this morning', and other wares for sale came out of what looked like a market lining the street.

"Okay." Simon took Callisra's arm and headed into the crowd. "Let's get to the port first. We'll figure how to not look nosy when we get there."

Madeline walked beside Jode as they wove through the crowds. Her mind was busy trying to think of a way to find some man who was probably not interested in being found. And how to do that in a strange city with no clue what the person looked like, or even if they really were a man. Zerenia said she didn't see enough to recognize them. It could be she'd seen women in disguise and not men at all.

The crowds and noise of the street recalled her life before Cartref, at least the fun of it. It had been a year since she was surrounded by so many people about their business. She felt comfortable in the hustle. She loved living in the Lower Plains, the small town that surrounded Jode's home – their home. But she missed the noise, the smells, and the sights of a bustling city. "I would like to come back here when we are done with this problem," she said.

He gave her arm a squeeze. "I was hoping we would go home after this. But, perhaps, a holiday by the sea will be good for our plans to have a child."

Madeline giggled and promised herself that she would take advantage of the nights, no matter how crazy the days were. Then a pang of guilt robbed her enjoyment. Every second they spent having fun, was more time that her friends would be under attack.

They turned a corner and the heat blew away on a salt flavored breeze. Madeline gazed at the line of boats tied at the dock. Instead of four or five large boats, the dock was crowded with hundreds of small ones, some filled with cargo and sitting so low in the water they were almost below the dock, others riding high as they prepared to shove off for more cargo. Following the line out to the horizon, Madeline saw two huge ships anchored almost beyond sight. "Wow," was all she could manage to say.

"I remember this," Callisra said. "The ships stay out because it is faster to unload and ferry the cargo to port than to maneuver them in each time. This way the tides are not as big a factor and more than one ship can be unloaded at a time."

Madeline tore her eyes from the waterfront and looked around. "Okay, where do we start? The bars?"

Facing the water were large warehouses, each defined a block with a grouping of tables and chairs spilling from just beyond the corner. Madeline noticed each row of tables and chairs extended halfway back to the doors of a bar. Their street seemed the only one that didn't cater to drinking and whatever else went on in the taverns of The City.

"Have you given thought to what questions we will ask?" Jode guided her to the closest pub.

"Yes, I think it would be best to start talking about Arabela and the Summer Lands. Then we can see if anyone bites at the conversation." She wished again that they had at least a description more than 'probably a man'.

Simon pointed to the first corner. "I think we can split up. I can go in as an entertainer and strike up some conversations. Callisra comes with me. You two can go in different places and talk to people." He gestured farther along the dock. "We'll go down four more streets. In an hour, we'll all meet here. Sounds good?"

They split up and Madeline followed Jode into the pub. Sitting at the only empty table, they ordered tea.

"I hope that Arabela is doing well," Madeline said, ensuring her voice carried.

Jode nodded and glanced around. "Yes, a war in the Summer Lands would be very bad for trade."

No one paid any attention to them; and no one was obviously trying not to pay attention. Madeline drank her tea quickly and motioned for Jode to do the same. She lowered her voice, "Let's not waste time here. These people are more interested in the contents of their glasses than in our conversation."

At the next bar, they managed to interest a few patrons in a discussion about the effects of a war on the other side of the mountains, but no one offered even a hint of information about someone starting a war.

They stepped out into the brightness of the docks. "This isn't working," Madeline said. "We need to think of something else."

"Don't be impatient," Jode said, looking toward the next street. "This is a good plan. But, perhaps, drinking tea is not making us fit into the clientele."

She sighed and told herself to listen to her husband. It was more important to find this attacker than to do it quickly. "How will we do that without getting drunk? If we have to drink a beer at every place, we'll be asking people outright before too much time passes. And it's a bit early for drinking."

Jode stepped aside to glance down the street. "We will take turns. I will —"

"Look out!" A voice broke through Jode's words. He grabbed Madeline and pushed her aside. A flash of yellow caught her eye as it flew past where she was standing.

Jode spun away and Madeline turned to the sound of running, reaching for her throwing knives. This time she was ready to fight back.

The man striding toward her was tall and lean. She saw brown hair falling in waves to his shoulders, and as he came closer, hazel eyes shining with concern. The man was too relaxed to be on the attack and his face held nothing but worry, so she relaxed her stance.

A quick movement in the corner of her eye drew Madeline's attention for a second. A small man, an elf, slipped around the corner of the building to her right. She moved to follow him, but the brown-haired man stepped in her way.

"Are you all right?" he asked as he came to her side, dodging Jode who was reaching for her.

"I saw the yellow gull and shot it without thinking. I must apologize; the damn bird should have fallen to the ground. I clearly failed to kill it and now it is flying away with my best arrow."

Madeline held up her hand to stop Jode from retaliating. "No harm done. I am fine."

"That is a relief at least," the man responded. "Please allow me to introduce myself. I am known as Regis of the Downs."

"I am Lady Madeline of the Lower Plains and this is —"

"Jode of the Lower Plains." Jode stepped forward to shake hands, putting himself between Regis and Madeline. "I have not heard of the Downs."

Madeline watched as Regis' smile faded for a second, and then he regained his charm. "I have not been home for many years, but I am sure it is still in the same place." He looked to the north. "It is near the elven homeland. Not many people have heard of it."

Jode seemed ready to say more, but before he could, Callisra and Simon ran up. Madeline made the introductions, keeping her eyes on Jode, looking for a clue about why her husband seemed so tense. The set of his shoulders and the fact that he was positioned to keep his own body between Regis and Madeline was evidence of his suspicion, but she couldn't figure out why he felt the need to protect her; the bird had been an accident.

"Allow me to treat you to luncheon," Regis said, waving his hand toward a side street. "I know an exquisite establishment only steps away from the water. The cook is a dear friend of mine."

"We have a mission to complete," Jode said. "Thank you but we must return to our duty."

Madeline reached for Jode's arm to stop him from continuing. This man could be a great source of information.

Regis beamed. "But, surely, you must eat. And I am intimately familiar with all the inhabitants and secrets of The City. Perhaps I can assist in whatever endeavor you are about. Please, I feel the need to make amends."

Madeline didn't give Jode a chance to say no again. "I think that will be perfect. I would appreciate any help we can get."

As they followed Regis to the restaurant, Madeline held Jode back far enough to whisper, "What is wrong? He seems like a nice person."

"It is too much of a coincidence. He may have tried to kill you. I think he is too helpful. And how does he know we need assistance anyway?"

"Well, I didn't feel a warning from my magic, so I think he's harmless. I suppose you might be right, he's a stranger after all. I do think you are exaggerating, but we can be careful. I won't tell him anything, but don't stop him telling us any gossip just because you don't like him."

"I will agree to let him prattle on, but first make sure he tells us more about himself." Jode put his arm around her shoulders and continued, "Perhaps I can dismiss this feeling that he is too much like a gift."

Madeline looked at Regis who was chatting with Simon. She sent her power out to touch his being. She felt a confusion of talents and colors before Regis turned and raised an eyebrow at her. Blushing, she said, "I apologize."

"No need, perhaps we can discuss our powers over the meal. I am unfamiliar with the feel of yours." He opened the door to a quiet room filled with tables covered in pristine white cloths. "It is always exciting to learn about the different magic others can touch, don't you think?"

Madeline's curiosity responded with a smile. It was refreshing to find someone who shared her passion for knowledge. The waiter showed them to a small table in the back of the room. After the waiter announced the specials, Regis asked permission to order for the whole party.

"Now, tell me about yourselves," Regis said, turning to Simon and Callisra. "You are newly wed, yes?"

"How did you know that?" Callisra asked. Madeline recognized a twinge of suspicion in her tone. Was she the only one who took Regis at face value? Was she being naive?

Regis beamed. "Ah, the love you have for each other shines for anyone to see."

Madeline turned the conversation back to her own interests. If she could get him started on magic, it would be easy to shift to finding someone who could cast magical attacks. "Regis, I would love to hear about your magical powers. They felt so different from any I've encountered before. I thought people only had one type, but I felt at least two when I touched yours."

The waiter placed plates of vegetables and seafood on the table and added two bottles of wine. When he left, Regis poured the wine and said, "I am fortunate enough to possess three powers. One I believe is the same as yours; I cast my magic with my mind. But I am also able to use a device; I favor beads when I am tired."

Madeline played with the food on her plate. "And you have more than that."

"Yes." His smile faded a fraction before returning at full wattage. Madeline was not sure it had happened at all. "But I felt something different when you touched. What was that?"

The fade of his smile had raised Madeline's suspicions enough to make her cagey. "I don't know. My power is what it is."

Simon raised his glass for a refill and asked, "What do you do here in The City, Regis?"

"Oh, this and that," he said airily. "I have friends who need favors and are generous when I take care of these favors. And I am fortunate at the card tables. Perhaps I can do you some favor that will assist you in this mission."

Everyone glanced at Madeline. She was thankful that they let her manage the conversation, but at the same time it was a lot of pressure. "What makes you think we have a mission?"

"It is clear by your actions that you are searching for something. Your husband here is all seriousness and that means it is not a casual something." His eyes narrowed for a second. "And he mentioned a mission only moments ago."

Madeline settled back in her chair. "We are looking for someone. I don't know who they are."

Regis gave a graceful nod. "That is a difficult task in The City. It is a place where many come to hide. Perhaps if you tell me what you know, I can help."

Jode shifted in his chair and Madeline glared at him. This was not the time to put up obstructions. "This person is a powerful mage," she said. "Do you know any mages?"

A shadow passed over Regis' face, and then he waved it off. "There are several who live here or spend time here. Is this person human?"

Jode answered before Madeline could. "We believe it is a man, but perhaps not human."

"I know of one person who would fit that shoe," Regis said. "Eat and I will tell you about him."

Madeline took a forkful of the white fish from her plate. It was sweet and the coating crunched. The food was as promised, perfect. She hoped Regis' information would be as good.

"As you know." Regis waved an arm around the table. "We are not the only creatures who have magic in this town. Most species are represented if only in a merchant capacity. The Mariai welcome all who wish to trade and keep the peace. There are many who we know as enemies outside the walls and some, the Scree for instance, have increased their presence lately. It is something that concerns the Watch, but so far, no problems. And there are others who may slip under the eye of the officers of the Watch, but not many."

"We saw some Scree when we entered," Simon said.

Madeline sent him a look meant to stop him sharing more information about their adventures. "I assume these are keeping the peace."

Regis nodded. "I have not heard otherwise, but then one never knows with Scree."

Jode pushed his empty plate to the center of the table. "And, your information?"

Taking a sip of his wine, Regis paused. "Yes, well there are those you might think are allies here that are not. One such is a powerful mage elf. His name is Springheart and I suggest that you tread carefully as you uncover his involvement in whatever you are investigating."

Now that's what I call information. "Why? Is he dangerous?"

Regis waved away the suggestion. "Not anything that can be proven. But he has a reputation for, shall we say holding the truth close, when it should be shared openly."

AFTER LISTENING to Regis tell them interesting, but unhelpful, stories of The City for an hour, Madeline was happy to return to the inn. Resting through the heat of the late afternoon had helped restore some of her energy. She stood in the private courtyard outside their room at the inn. The shade was delightful compared to the baking she'd received on the docks. Turning to see Jode step through the French doors to join her, she said, "I thinking we need to change tactics."

He wrapped his arms around her and kissed her cheek. "It was not a productive day. What do you propose?"

She kissed him, and then wiggled out of his embrace. "I've been wondering who would want to take the Summer Lands.

Maybe if we knew more about Alric's family... could this be about something he did?"

"It might, but what about these attacks on us?" He drew her into one of the chairs facing the back wall of the courtyard.

Madeline inhaled the scent of the deep pink roses that climbed across half of the stonework. "I don't know what to think about that. It seems to have stopped, at least for now. Besides, I can only deal with one thing at a time." She snuggled into his arms. "We're capable of fighting off anyone who tries to attack, right?"

He chuckled and the vibration echoed through her body. "I suppose that is true. But do not forget that assassins do not always announce themselves, and they most certainly don't always miss. If you become careless..."

"I will never forget that feeling when I thought you were dead." She let out a breath and tried to send the sudden tension with it.

He kissed the top of her head. "Could you scry Blu and ask his advice?"

"No. I tried to see how far I could get a few minutes ago, and as soon as I approach the mountain, there is resistance, and then a wall I can't penetrate. Anyway, we talked before I left. If he has any new advice, he'll find a way to reach us."

"Well, let us join the others in the dining room and maybe something will come to us."

Dinner was laid out on a buffet. The other guests were settling into tables when Jode and Madeline entered. Simon waved them over to a table near the buffet. Madeline wondered how Zerenia managed to support the inn with so few guests. A couple of human men huddled over cups of wine, muttering a conversation. A Mariai family silently eating and a lone Eldman were the only other guests.

As Madeline sat, Callisra leaned over to whisper, "Why don't you ask Zerenia about Tadric. She might have a vision or something. Or, maybe, she knows someone who might know something."

"I know many people," Zerenia said, appearing behind Callisra as though summoned by the mention of her name. "What is it that you wish to know?"

Madeline gestured to an empty seat and Jode rose to pull out the chair. "Is it safe to talk here?" Madeline glanced around as she asked.

"Yes," Zerenia said. "My home is only open to those I can trust. You are welcome because Blu gave his word that you were trustworthy."

Madeline explained what they had done so far. "I had been hoping to discover a clue about why someone would do this, but I am at a loss."

Zerenia nodded and beckoned a servant to bring wine to the table. "You are hoping to learn something about who might think they are entitled to rule the Summer Lands."

Simon leaned toward Zerenia, and said, "What we know is that Alric was an only child. And only his son can inherit. Tadric was born after Alric was murdered, so is the only legitimate heir to the land. If he dies, anyone can lay claim, but will have to fight it out."

Zerenia gave a worldly smile. "And you are sure that Alric was faithful to Lady Arabela?"

Madeline felt Jode stiffen beside her. "Yes," he said, his voice tight. "He was my friend and I know he loved her with all of his heart. He would not have bred any bastards."

Madeline patted his leg to remind him they were asking for help and not a fight. "What about before they were together? Could there be another child from a previous lover?"

Jode shook his head. "He was careful. He did not wish to muddy the inheritance."

Zerenia poured a dark wine into tiny glasses. "This is a local drink, for the digestion. Sip it slowly or you will find yourselves unable to stand from the potency." She took a sip and closed her eyes with a smile. "Now, you seem to believe that whoever is attacking feels they have a right to rule the Summer Lands, correct?"

"Yes, but that might just be because that's the simple answer. If we have to put together a list of people who would just try to take over, it would start with all of the Scree and most of the Choi, and then perhaps Arabela has made some enemies." Madeline sipped and almost choked on the alcohol burn. "Are you sure this doesn't need diluting with water. Maybe ninety percent?"

Zerenia took another sip before answering, "No, but the first sip is the worst. You will notice the flavors with the next one. And the flavors are delicate."

Madeline glanced at Simon and noticed he had managed to half empty the glass. He nodded and she tried another tiny sip. This time her mouth filled with the lightness of apple blossom, citrus – and burning alcohol. "Yes, I see what you mean. It's refreshing."

Zerenia smiled. "Now, back to the problem of saving Tadric. I am sorry I have no vision for you, but I have logic, which may be better in this case. I think you are correct in your assumption. This must be someone who anticipates an easy take over. I can only think that means a lost relative. But, as memory serves, both of Alric's parents were only children. This relationship may be very tenuous."

"No, it must be clear," Callisra said. "Despite the attacks, this person thinks they will be accepted. That means they probably expect to be recognized. Perhaps this is not about what Alric has done; perhaps it is about his parents."

Jode pushed his empty glass to the center of the table and covered it with his hand when Zerenia lifted the bottle. "I think I prefer to keep a clear head, thank you. I knew Maltius and his was not a love match. Lenora was a bride chosen to settle a border argument and she was a hard woman to live with. Maltius was often away from home. But he would have been careful – he was the one who taught us to…" Jode looked away.

"Jode, don't worry I realize you had a life before we met." Madeline grinned; she had a life before as well. "Careful or not, accidents happen. Alric could have any number of half siblings." As she said it, her skin warmed with the itch of her magic. There was truth in her words. "No, make that does have siblings."

"So, the challenge is to find this bastard of the Summer Lands," Zerenia said. "Perhaps now that we have some information a vision will be made available. I will seek one tonight. But I will also ask certain… friends to find information."

She made her way back to the door, stopping to greet guests as she went.

Madeline turned to her husband. "Jode, do you remember any particular place Maltius traveled to frequently? Perhaps we can find someone who knew him."

"He came here," Jode said. "He would venture out on hunting trips around the Summer Lands, but he loved The City and it was here he came when he needed peace."

Madeline stretched her back and groaned. "I think an early night is in order. If Maltius came here and the attacks are coming from here, then it stands to reason we'll find the long-lost sibling here." She waited for her magic to confirm her words, but it was silent. "Well, this may be finished by the end of tomorrow. If there is a bastard, he should be easy to find."

4

$\mathcal{T}$he next morning Madeline knocked on Zerenia's door hoping that there was news. A maid opened the door and said, "My mistress is not seeing visitors today."

"Is she well?" Madeline hoped that the innkeeper was not suffering because she'd spent the night looking for visions.

"Tired, but that is all. I must go back to my duties." She smiled and closed the door slowly, trying to be polite while still cutting off anything Madeline had to say.

Madeline returned to the breakfast table where the others were waiting. "We are on our own, at least for now."

Callisra passed Madeline a mug. "Perhaps we can find some records of the Summer Lands' family. If Maltius came here frequently, some of the older residents may remember him."

"Great idea," Simon said. "Did you notice that the owners of the stores around this inn are ancient enough to have been here when the first stones were laid? We could start by dropping in and asking for news of The City."

Madeline was about to agree when the maid appeared at her shoulder. "Madam, there is a man wanting to see you."

Madeline looked at Jode and raised her eyebrow, no one

knew where they were staying. In fact, few people knew they were here at all. Jode asked the maid, "Do you know who this man is?"

She glanced over her shoulder as though trying to remember who was waiting. "No, sir."

Madeline shrugged. "Bring him here. There is plenty of privacy now that everyone else has finished breakfast."

While the maid went to bring their mystery guest, Madeline cleared a space at the table. "Do you think it's Regis?"

Jode was looking down the hall. "No. It is an elf."

Turning, Madeline saw the visitor emerge from the dark hall. About her height, he was thin and moved with the grace of a hunter. His blond hair hung straight to his shoulders. As he got closer, she noticed his eyes, intense and focused on her to the exclusion of the others, one eye blue the other brown.

"Lady Madeline, and your friends," he said, taking a bow. "I am sorry to intrude, but it is important I speak to you. I am known as Springheart."

Madeline remembered seeing the flash of an elf leaving yesterday when they'd met Regis. And she remembered Regis' warning. "I'm surprised you knew where to find us."

He cocked his head and gave a crooked smile. "I must admit I followed you yesterday. I hope I have not caused you concern."

Jode rose and moved beside Madeline. "Please, sit and join us. There is tea and pastry if you have not yet broken fast."

Madeline recognized the sound of a formal greeting ritual. She smiled and told herself to listen to what Springheart had to say regardless of what Regis had warned. Keeping an open mind wouldn't hurt, or at least they'd be prepared if he tried to hurt them. Her knives were always part of her outfit. Besides, they had been in The City for a whole day with little or no progress. If she didn't keep her mind open, she might miss something crucial.

When the elf had taken the offered seat, she poured tea and then waited. He delicately sipped and seemed to be waiting as well. Madeline glanced at Simon and Callisra. They were watching her. Great, now she was expected to know how to deal with an elf — the first elf she'd met. On a movie screen or in a book didn't count.

She decided to be direct. "You have something to tell us?"

He placed the mug carefully on the table and then slowly nodded. "You were attacked more than once on your journey to The City."

"Yes." Madeline shivered at the memory of the arrow striking Jode.

"I believe this was the Scree." He held up a hand as Madeline started to speak. "I cannot prove it yet. But shortly after you arrived, a small band of Scree joined the delegates."

"We knew this, but I don't know if we can make that connection. I have history with Sayer Goddard's tribe." *Well, if by history I mean I was responsible for the destruction of his family line.* "But I understand that there is no one left to declare vendetta."

"That is true, no family survives. But with the Scree there may be a family connection no one knows of," Springheart said. Despite the earlier eye contact, he kept his face averted. Madeline realized she didn't know if that was culture or coyness.

She wished she'd known more about Sayer before he died. "How do you propose we use this information?"

A smile flashed across his lips. "An excellent question. I do not suggest you provoke them. An angry Scree is a dangerous one. I advise you to be wary if they are in sight. And be wary when they are not."

"And how do we find out if they are the ones who attacked us?" She could feel her patience wearing out. "It is all well and good thinking it is the Scree, but we need to be certain."

Springheart raised his gaze directly up to Madeline's; she felt his power as she returned his stare. She sent out a small probe, wincing as it bounced off a shield that shone like chrome when it connected. He smiled in recognition of her power. "I have sent out requests to friends for confirmation."

"Is this city run on requests to friends?" The words were out before she could stop them.

"Yes. The delicate balance of peace here is supported on a lace of favors and promises." He turned the mug in his fingers as he considered his next words. "I would freely give you the information if I were to find the culprits. But I must admit to having an ulterior motive."

Jode shifted in his chair, but Madeline ignored whatever signal he was trying to give her. "I would feel more comfortable if I knew what that was."

Springheart kept his gaze on the mug as he sighed. "I have been sent to The City to find someone. I think that someone is you."

"Why?"

He placed the mug on the table and rose. "I came to see you hoping that I would know by being this close. It did not happen, and it is vital that I am sure before I speak any further. I will seek the proof you need about these attacks. I promise we will meet again." He bowed and left before Madeline could ask when or where.

"Interesting character," Simon said. "You know, he reminded me of David Bowie; the eyes."

Madeline was still staring down the hall. "He was kind of pompous."

"Madeline, don't judge him by that," Callisra said. "All elves speak in circles. You will find he loosens up a little when he knows us better. It just might take a long time to get to know us."

"I hope so," Madeline said. "Was that why he looked away most of the time? No eye contact with strangers?"

Jode was still watching the hall as though expecting Springheart to return with answers. "No, that was not why. I think he has more to hide than this mission he mentioned."

. . .

MADELINE STOOD in front of a doorway screened by a curtain of red and amber beads. This was the third store she was going into, and she desperately hoped it was going to earn her more than a cup of tea and a biscuit. They had split the street, each taking a side and direction. Jode and Simon would be almost at the docks by now. Glancing over her shoulder, she saw Callisra step out of a dry goods store across the street, pulling her hair off her shoulders to let the cooling air dry the sweat on the back of her neck before turning to walk to the next storefront.

Looking up her side of the street, she counted only four more stores in sight. Unless something changed, she would be back in the dining room in less than an hour. A cool drink and lunch would go a long way to offset all the sugar and caffeine. And maybe by then Zerenia would be out of her room.

This store had a sign that she couldn't read because it was covered in dust and there were no windows to give a glimpse of the wares. A faint waft of cinnamon and cumin identified it as a spice store. She pushed aside the beads and stepped into the dimness. The room was cooler than the street, but the combined aromas of familiar and strange spices made the air as rich as a winter stew.

"Yes, lady, what can I do for you this morning?" The voice came from behind a counter in the back of the store. A tiny man sat on a stool, a scroll in his hand.

Madeline smiled and started on her cover story. "I am helping a friend try to find her relatives." Close enough to the truth that it wouldn't matter when the merchants started talking about the people asking questions. "The Lady Arabela of the Summer Lands."

"And you think I may be able to help? I am not an archivist. I keep records of the movement of spices not the births and deaths of families." He climbed down from the stool. Madeline watched the top of his head as he moved around to the front of the counter to join her.

"I am known as Rymant," he said, holding out his hand.

"Madeline of the Lower Plains." Madeline introduced herself and reached out to shake his hand, but he turned it and kissed the back before releasing it. "I am hoping that someone on the street might remember Alric, or perhaps his father."

Rymant beckoned her to the back to of the store. "Ah, Maltius. Yes, I remember him. He was fond of a party and fond of the ladies."

Madeline followed Rymant through the store and prepared herself for another cup of tea. "So, you knew him well."

"Sit and we'll have a glass of this excellent beer." He called out as he passed through a room to a patio. "Samell, go watch the store." And a young woman hurried to the counter.

Madeline accepted the offered glass of dark beer. "You knew him? I admit he is a mystery to me."

"Oh, Maltius was a friend to everyone." Rymant pointed to the glass in Madeline's hand. "How do you like the beer?"

Madeline took a careful sip. The taste filled her mouth, rich sweet molasses, and bitter hops. "Refreshing."

Rymant settled back in his chair and nodded. "Good. Now, as I remember, Maltius was married and had one son."

"Yes, but we wondered if perhaps there was another child." Madeline reminded herself to be patient.

Rymant shrugged. "I know he was careful to avoid fathering a child because of the possibility of muddying the inheritance. I believe he was faithful to his marriage contract, if not to his wife."

Madeline sighed. If that was true, then their search was useless. "It seems the family runs to only children in one way or another."

Rymant was lost in thought and didn't respond. Madeline was about to prompt him when he looked up at her and continued, "But there was one woman that I remember." Rymant frowned and tapped his glass in thought. "She was a favorite of his. From the north, she was. A pretty thing, but I worried that he spent too much time with her."

Madeline felt the pull of a real lead. "Is there anyone we can ask for more details?"

"No one that comes to mind, but I will think on it. I am sure I don't need to caution you to be careful who you ask for information." He waited until Madeline nodded. "Well then, you may have some luck at the gaming houses. Maltius was fond of a gamble, and was lucky enough to be skilled at winning."

Unwilling to let the clue slip away, Madeline asked, "What did this woman look like? If we had some clue..."

"Let me see what I can find, but do not get your hopes up. Careful as he was, Maltius was with many women, some elves, and of course, some Mariai. I think if there were another child, we would know already. Do you not think so?"

Madeline had wondered the same thing. If there was a real heir, why did they wait until now to do anything?

Before she could speak, the young woman scurried onto the patio. "Grandfather, the pepper seller has arrived for his appointment."

He rose and said, "I must go meet with him. Lady Madeline, I will see what I can find out for you. Where are you staying? If I do have news, I will send Samell to find you."

Madeline finished the last sip of her beer and followed Rymant to the front of the store. Leaving her room number, she stepped out into the glare of the street.

Standing on the street deciding on whether to go back to the room or try one more store, Madeline noticed Springheart leaving the inn. She hurried toward him, thankful for a reason stop her search. "Were you looking for me?"

"Yes, and I am happy to have found you." He gave a small bow. "I have found some information about the Scree."

"Come in and tell me. The others should be back soon." She

led him to the dining room where the servants were setting up for lunch.

They settled at a table and Springheart took out a small notebook. "I have confirmed that just after you entered The City, a party of Scree arrived. They are staying at the house of the Scree ambassador and have not left since."

Madeline had expected a more flowery delivery. "Is that everything?"

"No. I have also discovered that the Scree who followed you into The City are from the Goddard clan, by mating ritual. Is that important?"

Madeline nodded. "Yes, they have reason to be angry with me." She knew that the Scree would not forget the fact that she'd been the cause of Sayer Goddard's death, and the death of his children. "This is good information, Springheart. Thank you."

His smile was a bit too smug for her to like the elf, but perhaps he was going to be useful.

He glanced toward the door before saying, "Take care how you use the information. I still believe you are the reason I am here, and I would hate to put you in danger."

Madeline groaned inside. She really didn't need another quest, or whatever this elf thought she was fated to do. Maybe he was mistaken. Maybe she could convince him he was looking for someone else. "Tell me more about yourself, Springheart."

He accepted a glass of tea from one of the servants and sipped before answering. "I come from deep in the elven lands. I am a wanderer. A man with no home."

"Do you wander everywhere? I mean, how do you decide where you will go?" Madeline couldn't seem to form her question clearly, but she knew so little about the elves it was hard to know what questions to ask.

"I was born outside the elven lands and that means I have no home. My mother was trying to get to her family, but I came early." He looked away as he spoke and Madeline saw his features firm as though taking control of his emotions.

"If I have asked questions that were too personal, I apologize. Perhaps you can tell me more about why you think you need me."

He stood and bowed. "I would love to speak more about this. Unfortunately, I am late for an appointment. Perhaps tomorrow?"

Madeline stood. "Yes. Tomorrow evening?"

"I will send a message with time and place."

"I AM NOT sure we can simply walk into a gaming house and start asking questions," Jode said as they sat in their room resting up for the evening. "We will have to join the players and that means putting money at risk."

Madeline finished wiping a cool cloth across her face and shoulders. Gambling was not really her skill. Even the slot machines at home weren't interesting enough to keep her attention. She wouldn't pass up this opportunity to get information. Every day that passed increased the feeling of dread. The heat kept them from spending every minute on their search. Without rest, she worried that she would pass out. "Do you gamble?"

"I have spent some time at cards, but I am not very good at it. Perhaps Simon has skills?" Jode kissed the back of her neck. "Or, perhaps we simply agree on the amount we will lose in pursuit of information?"

Madeline shook her head; Simon had many talents she knew nothing about, but it could get expensive if they didn't have any skills. "I wish Zerenia would come and tell us something. I just don't know that spending a night gambling with strangers is going to give us what we need. Do you even know where to find a gaming house?"

She turned so Jode could lace up the back of her dress. He tightened the laces enough to keep the dress in place, just enough room to breathe, but not enough to relax. She shivered when he placed another gentle kiss on the back of her neck.

"I would rather find someone who can act as our escort. What about Regis? He said he makes a living gambling." Jode kissed her again.

"I didn't think you trusted him." Madeline turned in his arms and pulled him close. "If we keep this up, I don't know if I will want to leave."

"As tempting as that is," he said, kissing her forehead. "We must stop these attacks on the Summer Lands."

She stepped away as he opened his arms. "I know. Let's go find out how to contact Regis, or find our own way to the gambling houses."

While she waited for Jode to get the information, Madeline knocked on Zerenia's door. The same maid opened the door slightly and shook her head. "My mistress is still searching the visions for you."

"Is this usual?" Madeline worried that Zerenia needed their help and no one knew it.

"No, but it is not unknown. She tells me in the moments she surfaces that there is a barrier and that there are many eyes seeking knowledge." The girl smiled. "Do not worry. She will find an answer."

Madeline thanked the maid and returned to Jode who was waiting in the lobby. Simon and Callisra had joined him and the three of them were talking quietly.

"Well, are we going?" she asked.

Jode broke off his answer to something Callisra had asked to say, "The kitchen boy has been sent to find Regis. The butler suggests we will need an introduction and Regis is the ideal person to do that."

"It is good to hear that I have my uses." Regis' voice called from the street. "I think a night off from your searching is a wonderful idea. I am pleased to be of service."

Madeline wondered why Regis had been so quick to appear. She decided to put it down to good luck and hoped it would follow them through the evening. "Thank you, Regis, we would have been lost without you. Is it far to the gambling house?"

He strode toward her. Dressed in a red jacket that shone like silk, over tight blue trousers, he waved a hand as though dismissing the thought of traveling. "Only a street or two away. Far enough that we will have the chance to show off our finery, but not so much that we will wilt before arriving. You all look perfectly turned out for the night. Ladies, you will be the toast of the tables."

Jode stepped forward as Regis reached them. Madeline was amused at the show of jealousy until Simon joined him. Both men creating a wall between their wives and the intruding male. Stifling a giggle Madeline glanced at Callisra hoping to share her amusement. Her friend had not moved, but she looked happy to be protected. What was it about Regis that made the men so protective? She put aside the question for later. Tonight, they needed Regis feeling helpful not defensive. Stepping forward, Madeline placed her hand on Jode's arm and said, "It sounds like a lovely night. I am looking forward to meeting new people and learning the local games."

"Indeed," Regis answered. "Then we must leave soon. The tables fill quickly and you will be left with only the beginners to play with."

Madeline took Callisra's arm and gestured to the door. "We would not like that. Callisra and I will follow while you men discuss the strategy for the evening. Let's hope we win more than we bet."

The gambling house was just that, a house. Madeline would have walked by without giving it a second thought if Regis had not been guiding them. Plain on the outside, it was just another adobe building in a row of them. As soon as they got inside, Madeline was dazzled by the bright glow from what looked like a thousand candles, all set on, or in front of, mirrors. The heat of the lighting was drawn away from the gamblers by lazy fans circling on the ceiling.

Tables were scattered around the large front room. Most were full of people bent over cards or dice, so focused on the games that they were oblivious to anything else. A grand staircase curved down from the second floor to the center of the room. Servants moved quickly to carry full trays up to the second floor, and empty ones down. A small group of musicians played quietly on a balcony, the music just loud enough to soften the noise from the tables.

"I must introduce you to our host first," Regis said as he led them to a large door to the right of the stairs. "After that, I have some commitments to fulfill, but we will arrange for you to play as you wish. Then we will meet again at the end of the evening to compare notes."

Their host was a Mariai man tattooed all over his face. He didn't speak to them, but simply nodded at the introduction. He flicked a glance at all four of them and then reached into a case of chips. He held out four black chips and one green.

Regis interpreted the gesture, "It is customary for the first game to be funded on the house. Once you have lost that, you must play with your own money. The black chips will buy you into any game. The green chip is entrance to the training table."

As they reentered the central room, a servant stopped them and presented glasses of effervescent red wine.

Madeline looked around the room but could not decide where to start. "Can you tell us what game to join?"

Jode pointed at a table where four men were tossing dice onto a brilliant green cloth. "Simon and I will start with the battle dice. We have had enough practice with the musicians."

"Excellent choice," Regis said as they wandered toward the table. "Now, I will be playing cards in one of the private rooms. I regret I cannot invite you. Ladies, if you are not familiar with the games, there are lessons to be had in there." He gestured to a space behind the stairs. "Simply present the green chip. It will do for both of you."

"Callisra?" Madeline had no idea if her friend gambled.

"Oh, I will join a game of fates," she replied pointing to a lively group near the fireplace. "I think it would be a good idea if you took advantage of the lessons. When you are more comfortable, you can find me there. I promise not to leave for another game without letting you know. With fates, you never know what I'll find out between rounds." She winked at Madeline before joining the game.

"Now, before I leave you," Regis said. "Tell me what information you are trying to obtain. I will do my best to find out what I can."

Madeline knew that it would not be long before everyone in town knew they were looking for information on Maltius, so she didn't feel the need to be discreet. "We would like to talk to someone who knew Maltius of the Summer Lands."

Regis' smile didn't reach his eyes this time. He gave a slight bow. "I never met him myself, of course. He died when I was very young. But I am testing my luck and skills against some venerable players tonight. I am sure we will be able to find someone who knew him. Well, good luck. I will see you in a few hours. We can share our knowledge over supper."

Madeline felt optimism replace lingering weariness as she headed toward the lessons table. When she found the training table, she realized she would need to learn fast and rejoin the main room. No one at the table looked older than fifteen. They would not even know Maltius existed.

THE EVENING HAD BEEN FUN, but uninformative. Madeline suppressed her resentment at the thought of so much time wasted. In the moment there had been enjoyment, now she simply wanted to move on to the next action. She took off her jewelry, placed it on the top of the dresser, and then laid the coins she'd won beside her earrings. "I'm sorry you weren't so lucky," she said to Jode. "I'm more sorry we didn't find anything out about Alric's father."

"It looks to me like you won almost as much as I lost." He unlaced her dress and turned her to face him. "It troubles me more that Regis was not able to introduce us to any of the old guard. We will have to try another way." He kissed her then helped her out of the dress.

Madeline didn't relish the idea of spending another evening playing cards. "I felt like I was missing some important social grace all the time I was playing. Like everyone was laughing at me as I played."

"I did not notice anyone laughing when you took their money," Jode said. "I'm sure there is another way. We will solve this."

"Yes. I know we will, eventually. I just want it to be sooner rather than eventually." She slipped into her nightdress and joined Jode in bed. "Maybe we should tell Regis exactly what we've learned so far. He seems to know everyone. I'm sure he'll find out what we need in no time at all."

Jode drew her close before saying, "I know you like him, but I feel he is not to be trusted."

"Why do you think that?" Madeline drew away from him. "I don't like him. I don't dislike him either."

"I think you trust him too much for how little we know about him," Jode said. "But let us not allow Regis to come between us."

Madeline let the anger go and wrapped her arms around his shoulders, pulling him toward her, relishing the sense of balance he brought. "Yes, I prefer it when we are alone in our bedroom."

Jode chuckled and kissed her, loosening her night dress so that it slid to the floor. Just as Madeline reached to remove Jode's shirt, someone knocked on the door.

"Just a moment," she called, reaching for her cloak.

Jode went to the door and waited for her to nod before opening it.

Zerenia's maid stood in the darkness of the hallway. Madeline's heart leapt. Perhaps the innkeeper had finally emerged from her vision.

"There is a man here to speak to you, lady," the maid whispered. "I told him it was not appropriate, but he insisted."

Madeline pulled her cloak closer. "Do you know this man? Is he young?"

The maid shook her head. "No, not young, old. I know him, though, he is the spice merchant."

"Ask him to wait." Madeline glanced around for some clothes. "Can you offer him tea?"

"Yes, Lady." The maid curtsied and hurried to the front of the inn.

Madeline pulled her tunic and a pair of pants from the trunk and turned to Jode. "This could be it," she said. "He could have a name for us. It's possible we'll have this resolved soon."

Jode pulled a sweater over his head. "Don't get your hopes up too high."

Madeline opened her mouth to tell him not to be such a party pooper, but his face was so full of concern she melted. "I will try, but I'm frustrated as hell about this. And we need a break."

As they passed Simon's room, Madeline thought to invite them. Then a giggle escaped and she decided to let the newlyweds have their fun.

The dining room was dimly lit by a single candle on the table where Rymant sat, a mug and pot of tea in front of him.

"Thank you for coming," Madeline said. "It is very late."

"I do not seem to need so much sleep these days," Rymant murmured. "Who is this?" He pointed to Jode.

Madeline introduced them and waited until hands were shaken and greetings exchanged. "You have news?"

Rymant smiled. "I do and I will be as direct as you. There was a child. A boy child."

Madeline waited, but Rymant added nothing.

"Do you know who it is, or a description?" Madeline tried to keep the impatience from her voice.

"The person who told me about this could only describe a boy child. Children change as they grow. This child would be thirty-one, or two, now." Rymant sipped the last of the tea in his mug. "I hope this information is of help. I should go now. I must open the store in only a few hours."

Madeline stood and said, "It will help, thank you. Let my husband walk you home. It is late, or should I say it is very early."

When Jode returned, Madeline was already under the blankets. "We have a place to start," she said throwing the covers aside to let him in.

"Yes, but what do you think we can do with it? I asked Rymant who gave him the information, but he would not tell me. Apparently, this person does not want it leading back to them. We cannot interrogate every male in his early thirties in The City."

"Well, no, but we at least we know who it can't be. That's something."

He drew her close. "Yes, but you know that not all people show their age."

Madeline snuggled into his arms. "Let me enjoy this. I know it's not much, but it's a start. We'll figure out how to use it in the morning."

5

The next morning, Madeline woke early and sat up in bed. Then she threw off the covers and ran to the bathroom.

"Are you unwell?" Jode called after her. "Should I call Callisra?"

Madeline didn't answer other than to slam the door shut. She fought the nausea as long as possible but it didn't subside until she had emptied her stomach into the bowl.

"Oh my god," she whispered, settling back on the floor. "What the hell was that?" She wiped the chilled sweat from her brow.

When she stood, she felt a little dizzy, but the worst of it had passed. She rinsed her face and looked in the mirror.

"Madeline," Jode shouted through the door. "Are you all right?"

"Yes," she said weakly. "Just a minute."

Opening the door, she tried to smile her reassurance, but his eyes widened in shock. "You look near death." He picked her up and placed her on the bed. "I will get Callisra. No. Do not fight me on this, Madeline."

She shook her head, not wanting to speak as the nausea took

over again. As soon as Jode was out of the room, she ran to the bathroom and slammed the door.

When she returned to the bedroom, Callisra was waiting. "Jode, go and have breakfast with Simon. I don't care if you are not hungry. Leave us alone so I can see what is wrong with Madeline."

Jode looked at Madeline, fear on his face. "I will remain if you want me to, my love."

"Go, I'm sure it's nothing. I'll survive." When he hesitated, she kissed his cheek and said, "I promise Callisra will come get you if I am about to die."

He bent and kissed the top of her head. "Do not even joke about that." He turned and gently closed the door behind him.

"Simon was also ill this morning, but recovered quickly. How bad is it for you?" Callisra asked as she went to the bathroom and retrieved a clean damp towel.

"It was sudden. I woke up and everything slid sideways. I felt better for a little while, but then it happened again." Madeline waited, but the nausea seemed to have left for good.

Callisra wiped her patient's face with the towel. Madeline felt her cold clamminess recede with the tender care.

"Did you eat anything that we didn't?" Callisra asked as she placed a hand on Madeline's brow. "Although I should ask if you and Simon ate anything we did not."

Madeline shook her head.

Callisra sat back and placed the towel on the end of the bed. "It is unusual for it to take so long if it is a problem with food. It may be the stress of this quest we are on. Or perhaps an insect. Were you bitten in the night?"

"That's an inappropriate question," Madeline said and then giggled.

Callisra laughed with her. "If you are joking then you must be feeling better."

"A little. And I'm starting to feel hungry," she said. "In fact, now I mention food, I'm starving. Maybe it was the stress."

"Then it is probably nothing. Let me check you for bites just in case. I'm sure you've purged the poison, but just to be sure."

Madeline patiently stood while Callisra examined her skin from toe to scalp. She found nothing.

"I can sense your health if you want. But if you are feeling better, I'm inclined to think it was a passing thing. You have no fever and you are feeling hungry."

Madeline started dressing. "I am more than hungry. Let's join the boys for breakfast."

When they walked into the breakfast room, Jode rose and rushed to Madeline. "You are well. Thank you, Callisra."

"I did nothing, Jode. She is very strong."

Madeline kissed her husband, and then started filling a plate from the buffet.

Over breakfast, Madeline and Jode updated the newlyweds. "So, we need to figure out how to narrow the options from every thirty-year-old male to the one who is attacking Arabela and Tadric."

Simon spread butter on a toasted bun and shared half of it with Callisra. "I guess we're certain that the attacker is this..." He turned to Callisra. "What would you call it?"

"Bastard heir," she answered.

"Okay. I thought it would be a little less brutal, but bastard it is," he said. "So, if we only look at motive we've got the bastard. I guess motive is all we have anyway. Are you sure he will be a human? Didn't that old guy say Maltius had a fling with an elf woman? Are elves and humans capable of producing offspring?"

Callisra swallowed a bite of the bread and answered, "Yes, most beings that look human can cross breed. It is rare, because the offspring are unpredictable, particularly when it comes to magic."

Madeline felt the tenuous hope from last night slip away as

the discussion continued. "We can toss around ideas all day until we end up doing nothing. Why don't we start with the assumption that this is a human? If it doesn't pan out, we can expand the search. But at least we can do something."

Jode patted her knee before saying, "I agree, but don't be discouraged by discussion. It is the way to open ideas."

"I know," she said on a sigh. "I'm sorry. I know all of this. Look, we still have Zerenia. She'll eventually come out of her room and maybe tell us something."

"No," Callisra said. "Be more positive. She will tell us something."

Madeline nodded and refilled the tea mugs. "I'll be happier when she comes out either way. I'm worried that she's in trouble, but there's nothing we can do about that."

"We have enough to worry about without adding imagined problems," Jode said.

"Speaking of things to worry about," Simon said. "What about the other attacks? Wasn't that Springheart guy supposed to come back with something on the Scree?"

"Springheart will come to you when he needs something," Regis announced as he entered the room. "Do not expect him to cater to your needs. I hope you are enjoying a good morning and not suffering from our late evening?"

Madeline smiled up at Regis. "We are all fine this morning. Join us for breakfast." She heard Jode snort out his displeasure. "We were discussing our plans for today."

"I am delighted to share a meal with you." He sat between Madeline and Callisra. "Now, before we discuss what you will do with your day, tell me what problem you have with the Scree. Perhaps in the absence of our half-elf, I can provide the information you need."

. . .

"IT IS HIGHLY probable that the Scree are attempting to exact revenge," Regis said as he finished his last breakfast pastry. "I have heard that the younger Scree have taken to avenging even imagined insults. They say there are no longer enough wars to satisfy their blood lust."

Madeline closed her eyes to find her peaceful beach. If the Scree wanted her to fight, they were just going to have to wait until she'd solved Arabela's problem. "I'm assuming they will be careful not to attract the attention of the watch. We have other, more pressing, business to deal with."

Regis emptied his tea mug and rose. "I will do what I can to find you information on our Scree visitors, but be careful. Your assumption is correct only as long as the threat of arrest is present. It would be a pity to lose you simply because someone pulled you into a darkened room and slit your throat."

Madeline saw Jode reach for his sword and patted his hand to calm the fury she could see burning in his eyes. "I appreciate that, Regis."

He executed a small bow. "As to your other business, let me suggest you visit the western parks. It is a pleasant neighborhood. But more to the point, there are older residents there. People who enjoy a good gossip in the park. Perhaps someone will remember your friend's father."

When he was gone, Simon rose from the table. "I'm not keen on him. He seems helpful, but is never any help."

"That last bit about the Scree sounded like a threat to me," Jode said.

"It was an odd way to put it, but he seems to be trying to help," Madeline said. "It's not like we've had any success with our other attempts."

Jode stood and gestured for Madeline to join him. "I think you were very successful. We know there is a male child which we didn't know until you talked to the spice merchant."

Madeline sighed. "I suppose. Maybe if we can get Regis to

sit and talk for more than ten minutes, we can get more out of him. I'm really curious about his powers, too. Have you ever heard of someone who can do magic in more than one way?"

"No," Jode answered. "And I don't like the idea that it can happen. Too much magic ability is not good for the character."

They stopped in the lobby to ask directions to the western parks. "It is a good day to seek the coolness of the parks," the doorman said. "You will need a carriage. It is much too far to walk there."

While the doorman arranged for transportation, Madeline checked on Zerenia. "This afternoon," the maid answered. "She has returned to her body but must sleep."

Returning to join the others at the door, Madeline continued the conversation. "What do you mean too much magic is bad for the character?"

A black carriage pulled up outside the door. Madeline noticed two lean men standing where she'd expected horses. *It's a good job there are no hills here.*

Jode helped her onto the seat of the open carriage. "I mean if he does not have to work for what he needs, he will not value what he gains. More importantly, he will not value the work others put in to gain what they have."

"Magic is work," Madeline said, looking to Callisra for support.

Callisra laughed and slid aside so Madeline could join her on the seat. "I cannot take sides. Madeline, you are right that he hasn't done anything specific to make us suspect him, but Jode has a point. I am not sure Regis is entirely trustworthy. His skill with the cards is quite suspicious. It could be luck, or it could be luck he makes."

IT TOOK twenty minutes of negotiating tight corners and narrow alleys to get to the park. A maze of streets that no horses could have managed.

Madeline felt the green calm her eyes and her soul. Between the desert crossing and the orange and beige of The City, it had been days since she'd seen a blade of grass, or a leaf. The cool shade and fountain seemed to press the ever-present dust to the ground. A relief to her skin, lips, and throat.

"I remember this from when I was a child," Callisra said. "I never did find out how they managed to keep all of this so healthy in such a dry region."

Madeline stepped down from the carriage, staring at the expanse of lawn in front of them. The park must take up an entire neighborhood. Like Central Park in New York, it was bordered by buildings. But these weren't the urban skyscrapers she knew. These were estates, each sitting in its own patch of green. As if the park were battling the houses for dominance.

Madeline pointed to the stone bowl filled with abstract shapes, each one spouting mist, or a stream of water. "It must be on a natural water source. I can't imagine they would spend the effort on this if it wasn't naturally irrigated. Running pipes here, from wherever they get fresh water, would be hugely expensive."

Jode took her arm. "I think we should join the people around the fountain. It seems to be a gathering place. Perhaps we can strike up a conversation."

They strolled across the lush grass towards the fountain. It was not like the courtyard fountains in the rest of The City, not even the one at the gate was so exuberant in its shower of water. As they approached, Madeline could see mist floating across the walkway and children running through jets of spray from the shapes that now resolved into fish and dragons.

"Isn't that Springheart?" Simon pointed. "Talking to that group of old women."

Madeline followed Simon's hand. "Yes. Should we go over?" She shook her head. "Why am I asking? Of course we are going."

Springheart looked up from his conversation as they approached. "Ah, Lady Madeline and friends, I see you have found the jewel of our city."

Madeline smiled at him. "Springheart, it's good to see you. I have been hoping we would meet you before this."

"Yes, I apologize. I have been delayed." He stood and bowed to the women. "Allow me to introduce my companions, the sisters Gorelle and their cousin Viette."

Jode bowed and introduced Madeline, Simon, and Callisra.

"Oh, how delightful. We meet so few of Springheart's friends. You must join us," the older looking sister said. "And call me Eilein, my sister is Olieva. Springheart, dear, bring some more chairs." There were scattered chairs and small tables all around the fountain, as if The City was encouraging people to dally.

"Springheart tells us you were attacked when you entered The City," Olieva said, fanning herself as though she was caught up in the attack. "I hope nothing else has happened while you have been here."

"No, nothing other than meeting so many wonderful people." Madeline glanced at Springheart. "All sorts of mysterious and wonderful people."

"Well, I hope that continues to be true," Olieva said, then lowered her voice conspiratorially. "Now you are looking for clues as to who might be behind this attack, yes?" She seemed to be the spokesperson of the family.

"Yes, we would like to find out who. I do not relish the thought of leaving The City with this unresolved," Simon answered. "Our information leads us to think it is the Scree."

The women drew back in alarm, looking around as though expecting rampaging savages to burst out of the trees. Before any of them could speak, Springheart rose. "I must leave you for another appointment. I apologize, but it is critical."

"But," Madeline said, "we have had so little time to talk."

"To my enduring regret," he said before bowing over her

hand. "But I must attend to this business. Perhaps I can invite you to dinner tomorrow."

Madeline wondered if tomorrow he would have some other urgent appointment. "We would love that."

He gave a curt nod and then hurried toward the road.

"Our Springheart has many responsibilities," Viette said. "We do not see enough of him."

Madeline glanced at Jode before speaking, "We know so little about him. He is always rushing off."

Viette reached across and patted Madeline's hand. "You must get to know him, perhaps then you can tell us more. All we know is that he comes from deep in the Elven lands. He arrived here a month or six weeks ago, and has been busy on some quest since then."

Just when the attacks on the Summer Lands started. "How did you come to know him?"

"Oh. We knew his mother," Olieva said. "Springheart doesn't like to speak of his family, some kind of rift we suspect. But our mother and his, her name was Oakenspring, were great friends."

Madeline glanced around the park, stalling for time. She wondered if she could just jump in with her questions about Maltius.

"You know," Callisra said before Madeline decided. "We are looking for information on another person your parents may have known."

"Oh. If this person was in The City, it is quite possible they knew our parents. They knew all of the important people," Eilein said, her voice high and breathy. "Who is it you seek?"

"Maltius of the Summer Lands. We know his daughter-in-law," Callisra said.

Madeline sat back in her chair, happy to let Callisra take control of the conversation so she could simply observe the reactions.

"Oh, he was the object of many a girlish infatuation," Viette said. All three giggled and Madeline guessed that they were three of the crushes.

"But there were two favorites," Olieva added. "Remember, that pretty dancer. Oh, she was lovely. Those eyes, so big, and that hair. Oh, we all hated her beautiful red curls."

"I remember," Viette jumped in. "She went away suddenly. Told her manager she had to return to nurse her sick mother. I always thought she was going to be a mother and that's why she left. But then, perhaps not."

"And the other favorite," Callisra prompted.

"The elven maid. Such a scandal," Viette said on a gasp. "I heard she was taken back to her people and locked away for dallying with a married man."

"Maltius' marriage was just a convenience." Olieva waved her hand in dismissal. "I'm sure he was careful about offspring."

"Well, Olieva," Viette interrupted. "There is careful and there is sure. Maltius could only be careful. We don't know the truth about why the girls fled."

"Was there any?" Callisra raised an eyebrow.

"Offspring?" Viette finished for her. "Not that we knew for sure. As I said, I suspected, but there was no baby laid at his door. I'm sure he would have taken responsibility if there were. He was honorable."

Olieva giggled. "Oh, Viette, there is no honor in dallying outside your marriage, even if it is just political."

"It was all so long ago. He was such a nice and handsome man. I understand his son was too. Such a tragedy." Eilein sighed. "But then the Summer Lands family was cursed with tragedy."

Madeline hoped they would be able to avert the next tragedy and turn the luck of the family around.

WHEN THEY RETURNED to the inn, Zerenia's maid waited for them in the lobby. "My mistress invites you and your companions to a private dinner. Please come to her room in an hour."

Madeline thanked her and they continued on to the rooms. "Not much time to get ready," she said. "But I don't think we need to get all dressed up."

"I was hoping to wear my new dress," Callisra said. "I know I shouldn't be so vain, but we're in The City and I want to feel like it's different from home."

"And it doesn't hurt to get dressed up for your new husband either." Madeline smiled as she said the words. "Right, let's put on a bit of glamor tonight."

Simon laughed and said, "I guess that means we need to smarten up a bit too, Jode."

"Perhaps we will hear good news tonight," Jode said, opening the door. "We must be prepared to celebrate, and I don't wish to be outshone by two beautiful women on our arms."

A half hour later, Madeline looked in the mirror above the dressing table. Her hair was braided in a complex pattern that she'd learned from Arabela. The plain gold earrings dangling from her lobes complementing the warm auburn of her hair. A wipe of red paste across her lips and she was ready. Her new sapphire dress was simply cut, but perfectly made and it was as if the color was created just for her. If she could attract good news by simply preparing for it, she was prepared to hear the name of the attacker and that they would stop and... well perhaps she shouldn't expect the whole solution in one vision.

"I would have taken more than an hour to get ready in my old world," she said turning to Jode. Her heart stopped when she saw him. Dressed in tight black pants and a pure white shirt, he looked like he stepped off a romance book cover. "Wow, you look good enough to make me want to stay in tonight."

He laughed and walked over to kiss her forehead. "We can always come back to the room after dinner."

"I'd like that. Perhaps we will learn something from the vision that will allow us to take a night off. It's been slow, Jode, I just want to finish this and know Arabela and Tadric are safe."

"It's been a month since we spent an entire evening alone without worrying about someone in jeopardy." He gently pulled her from the chair and kissed her deeply. "I have missed all thirty of those evenings. It will be nice when we can relax."

"How long until we meet Zerenia for dinner?" Madeline whispered. Moments like this allowed her to forget, if only for a moment, that they were here to save Arabela and Tadric.

"Not long enough," he said, pulling away from her. "We should go now before it is too late."

Simon and Callisra were already waiting when they arrived in the lobby. "The maid said to wait until she came for us," Simon said. "It's all weirdly mysterious. I hope it's worth it."

"Zerenia has a reputation for strong visions," Callisra said. "When we were out talking to the shopkeepers, I asked about her." She waved away Madeline's objection. "I was careful. But I thought it was important since we've already acted on her advice."

"I suppose it is good to know." Madeline turned as the door to Zerenia's room opened.

"We are ready for you." The girl waved them through to the dimly lit room.

Madeline looked across the low table to see Zerenia curled up in an armchair, a warm blanket tucked across her lap. The woman looked like someone who had been ill for a very long time. Despite her frailness, Zerenia smiled and reached out to pat the seat beside her. "Sit next to me, Madeline."

They arranged themselves around the table and the maid poured wine before she did a little curtsy and left them.

"Please enjoy the meal. My cook has worked so hard to prepare these delicacies," Zerenia said, reaching for a small bun. "This food is what the royal court of ancient Mariai would dine on for special occasions."

Madeline took a small plate and collected one of the buns, a skewer of meat, and some pickled items that looked like squash. "It's like dim sum, but different food. Simon, remember that place we used to go to in Chinatown?"

Simon finished chewing his bite of sautéed mushroom. "You mean the place you took clients?" He laughed as she started to protest. "Don't worry, that world is behind us. The food is definitely delicious. I could eat this all day."

"Thank you," Zerenia said. She picked up her glass of wine before speaking again. "I am sorry that it has taken so long for me to come back from the vision world. I hope you have learned things in the meantime that help you."

Madeline nodded, but didn't offer what they had learned. "Are you usually so worn by the visions?"

"Not usually, but sometimes." Zerenia sighed as though the effort of speaking was enough to drain her energy. "This time I have struggled against some barrier I am not familiar with. As though someone knew what I was seeking. But do not worry yourself. I will be back to my strength in only a couple of days."

Madeline looked at her again. The pallor set Zerenia's cheek tattoos in relief as though they were carved rather than inked. It would surprise her if the woman recovered in a month of rest and care. But she'd seen many things that surprised her here. "If it would be of help, Callisra is a healer."

"I am happy to heal you, if you want," Callisra offered.

"No, you must not waste your talent on me." Zerenia waved her hand. "You may need your energy for more urgent cases."

Madeline felt her stomach cringe at the thought that one of them would be hurt enough to require Callisra's skill. "Did you see this—?"

Zerenia held up a hand. "You are impatient to hear my vision, yes?"

Madeline nodded and placed her plate on the table. "I am anxious to finish this quest."

Zerenia closed her eyes and began speaking. "It was difficult. Often the visions seem to be waiting for me at the gate to the land of dreams. Sometimes I must call them to me, and others I must search for the vision." Zerenia paused, a flash of pain crossing her face. "This time the vision was waiting, but as I approached something came between us. A shadow, but it became thicker as I approached. I became trapped in this... it was like honey, sucking at me. It held me for days. I felt as though I was drowning, slowly. Each breath I took filled my lungs with something other than air. I remember terror. I remember fearing I was never going to leave the land, that I would become a messenger delivering visions for someone else."

She seemed to slip back to the world where her visions came from. Madeline reached out and touched Zerenia's hand. "You are safe here."

"Yes," Zerenia said in a stronger voice. "When I finally emerged from the trap, I saw the visions waiting but they had moved away from the gate. I ran to them and they paused. I have returned with the information."

Madeline waited while Zerenia sipped her wine again. She glanced at the others and they looked as rapt as she felt.

"I saw the two men," Zerenia said. "I recognized them. It was Regis of the Downs and Springheart."

Madeline drew back and started to speak.

"You know them," Zerenia said. "Yes, I see it in your eyes. One of these men is attacking the Summer Lands and one is drawing you away from the attack. I do not know if that is to save you or for another purpose."

"Do you know who is attacking?" Madeline asked, hoping.

"No," Zerenia said. "Please eat. Try the lemon pies."

Madeline reached for one of the tiny pies and bit. The flavor of caramelized lemons flooded her mouth. She swallowed before saying, "It is as delicious as the other food. Please, thank your cook. I suppose we at least know that we have located the two possible culprits. I am sorry it was so difficult for you."

Zerenia patted her hand. "I am not finished. I must tell you only what I saw, because I do not know how to interpret it."

Madeline nodded and picked at another morsel of food while she waited.

"I saw both of these men flickering. It was as though they were walking through a hall of windows. When they were in the light of the windows all was bright and clean. As they walked into the darkness, it was frightening. Ah, that is a poor explanation, but the best I can do."

Zerenia collapsed back into the chair. Madeline reached for her hand, fear clutching at her. But despite her appearance, her skin was warm and her pulse was strong. "Callisra, will you check her out?"

Callisra knelt beside Zerenia's chair and took her hands. After a moment, she looked up and said, "She's fine, just sleeping. I feel the life force rebuilding within her as we talk. We should leave her to rest."

They gathered in Simon and Callisra's room after sending the maid to her mistress.

"So, what do you think?" Madeline asked.

"I don't like the flickering thing," Simon said. "I wonder who got in the way."

Jode leaned against the wall. "Do you think someone set a trap? It's possible that it was part of the vision."

Madeline hadn't considered that. "So along with the flickering, the barrier would mean what?"

"On the face of it," Callisra said. "This solution will be difficult and possibly dangerous, but not impossible. That the culprit is not going to be who we think it is. Perhaps, it is both of them, for different reasons."

Madeline didn't think it would be that easy. "What about the fact that we know it's either Springheart or Regis?"

"I think it is Regis," Jode said. "I know that you like him. But there is something about that man I cannot trust."

"I don't know why you think I like him. But, at least, he is talking to us. Springheart is always rushing off somewhere."

"But, my love," Jode started, and then held up his hand. "No, we will not argue about this here."

Simon laughed. "Since when have you seen that work? Look, we do need to hash this out, but I don't think we will get there tonight."

Madeline hated the fact that they were right. Now she couldn't continue the argument because of Simon, and she couldn't stop because Jode had told her to. "I think we can discuss this without fighting. I do think Regis is trying to help, but I can't test my assumption. He will know I am trying to probe. And I haven't a clue how to read an elf."

"If we don't know how to identify friend from foe, I think we should assume they might both be foe, rather than the other way around." Callisra started to take down her hair. "Madeline, I like Regis too, but he has not been any more help than Springheart when it comes down to it."

Madeline rose and beckoned Jode. *So much for attracting good news.* "Let's talk this over in our room and leave the newlyweds to their rest."

THEY JOINED Simon and Callisra two hours later in the dining room, no closer to agreeing on their trust of either man.

Madeline poured a glass of water and said, "I'm worried. Despite getting little bits of information, we aren't making any headway."

"Yes, we seem to be stalled," Jode said. "I expect that it will take time to find our villain, but then we will settle the problem fast. I will not say don't worry. I will say have hope."

Madeline warmed at the words. Jode was right they were

attempting everything they could think of. Perhaps dealing with one problem at a time would help. "I'd like to try to find Springheart. It would be nice if we could find out more about the Scree. It is kind of distracting to have a threat hanging over us."

Simon waved to the maid. "So, you've come around to the idea he might not be the bad guy?" He pushed a cup toward her. "You'll never guess what showed up today, caf. Apparently, a shipment arrived an hour ago. Would you like some?"

"No, just tea for me," Madeline said. The thought of caf, brought a reminder of the sickness, although a snack was probably a good idea. After the maid brought the drinks and a tray of meats and bread, Madeline continued, "I have not come around, but I'm willing to give him an opportunity to show he's a friend."

"And Regis?" Jode asked.

Madeline looked up from the sandwich she was making with a slice of the flat bread and some smoked meat. "What about him?"

"Are you open to the idea that he is not a friend?"

Madeline took a bite of the sandwich to avoid answering right away. Why did she think Regis was a good guy? She swallowed and reached for her tea, still trying to find an answer. Not having a reason to argue his innocence, she answered, "Yes, I'll entertain the idea."

Simon sipped his caf before saying, "I think we should head back to the docks this evening. Maybe we'll see Springheart or Regis there. It seems like a place where everyone eventually shows up. When you've finished, we can get started."

Madeline looked at her plate. She'd eaten two of the sandwiches and a half of a sweet bun. "I guess I'm ready. And I need the exercise."

6

*A*s they left the inn, Madeline saw Springheart ahead of them heading to the docks. "Don't let him get out of our sight," she said, speeding up. "I am going to get him to stop and tell us what he knows, if it kills both of us."

Jode chuckled. "Poor Springheart. Let us hope he has some news."

When they caught up, the elf was talking to one of the officers waiting to board the shuttle boat back to his ship. The conversation was animated and Madeline slowed, standing back and letting Springheart finish. Jode stepped between her and the argument which seemed about to come to blows.

"Should we stop them?" she asked.

"No, let them finish," Jode said. "I suspect we will not help if we interrupt."

As he spoke, Springheart gave a crisp nod and the officer turned to board the shuttle. Now that he was alone, Springheart turned to see them, a smile lighting his face. Madeline couldn't help but feel that he knew they were there all along.

"It is good that we have met," Springheart said. "I was about to come to your inn to speak. But I had..." he turned to look at the shuttle as it floated away from the dock, "business to take care of for a friend."

"I hope it was successful," Callisra said.

"Yes, it was at the end." He gestured to the right. "Please let us sit in the shade and speak."

He led them to a small square where men sat smoking pipes and drinking something dark in tiny glasses. In the center of the space was a sand garden. Madeline noticed that, unlike the Zen gardens she'd seen at home, this one was carefully sculpted with grains as small as sugar sand and as large as boulders. There would be no daily raking here.

They found an empty bench close to the desert garden. Madeline noticed tiny plants tucked between the crevices, red and blue blossoms giving off a faint fragrance like lemons.

Even this late in the day, the sun beat down on the docks. The only shade there was came from the buildings that bordered the square. When she sat, Madeline realized how hot the sun had been on her head. A wave of dizziness passed through her as she cooled, and then was gone.

"You have something to tell us?" Madeline asked as soon as they were settled. "Is it safe to speak here in the open?"

"Yes," Springheart said. "As long as we do not speak loudly."

"What is your news?" Jode asked.

Madeline glanced at her husband, wondering why he was being so direct. He gave a minute shake of his head and turned back to Springheart.

"I have news on two fronts," he said, shrugging off his jacket and laying it on the bench beside him. "I find the heat here enervating. In my land, the weather is kinder. I hear it is the same across the mountains."

Madeline waited. She was afraid he would simply find a reason to leave, as he had every other time they met.

"Let me explain what has happened," Springheart continued. "I have been attempting to prove that the Scree are behind the attacks on you as you traveled to The City. And I have been trying to ascertain if you were the person I was sent here to find."

"And have you made any progress?" Simon asked.

Madeline felt annoyed that everyone seemed to be jumping in before she could ask her own questions. It was as if they didn't think she would give him a fair hearing.

"I have, but I think it is important that I tell you something about why I am in search of someone here. I cannot tell you everything until I have confirmed that lady Madeline is the person, but I can tell you something."

"Is this what you made progress on?" Madeline asked quickly.

"A little."

Madeline tamped down her frustration at Springheart's apparent determination to be stingy with his information. "We have our own mission here. These attacks, whoever is behind them, if they continue, would impede us."

Springheart didn't answer. Madeline saw the flicker of his thoughts cross his face. This was one of the reasons she felt he couldn't be trusted. He considered everything. It made her feel like he was hiding something. Unlike Regis, who chattered on unthinking. Then again, perhaps his own mission was why Springheart had to consider his words.

He finally flicked a glance around and said, "I understand. I have found a contact in the Scree household who tells me the newcomers are here on a blood revenge."

"I thought there would be no repercussions," Madeline said, looking at Jode. "I thought you said it was over."

"Repercussions from what?" Springheart asked.

"I... well most of us, were involved in the death of Sayer Goddard." Madeline pushed away the memory of the woman she'd killed. "He was going to steal the Summer Lands from Arabela."

"I see." Springheart looked impressed. "I had heard that tale. So, you are the woman from another land."

Jode put his arm around Madeline's shoulders. "Yes. But Sayer had no family left to declare blood revenge."

"I will ask my contact for more details now that I know." Springheart glanced around again. "I understand it was not just Sayer that you killed."

"No, his child died, but that was an accident," Madeline said, her stomach turning at the memory of Sayer taking his son over the edge of tower. "And a woman."

"Thank you for the details," Springheart said, sympathy in his voice. "I know that killing, no matter how justified, leaves its marks. I caution you about leaving The City without proper protections."

"We will worry about leaving when we have finished our job here." Madeline pushed up the sleeves of her dress, as the sun sank, leaving behind the weight of humidity and heat. "Tell us about your mission, or what you can of it."

Springheart nodded. "I have been sent to The City by prophecy."

Madeline suppressed a groan. A prophecy was what had prompted Blu to bring her here.

Springheart didn't seem to notice her reaction. "There is great danger to Cartref coming."

Of course, there was. Why waste a prophecy on something insignificant? Madeline tried to keep her irritation out of her voice. "What did the prophecy actually say?"

Springheart laughed. "I see you have experience with such things. How much do you know about the elven tribes?"

"Little to nothing. You are the first elf I've met."

"Perhaps I can give you a few details first," he said and waited for her nod. "The elders of our tribes are connected to the next life more than they are to this one. We do not call prophecy, it calls us."

"Your elders sit around all day waiting for prophecy?" Madeline regretted the question as soon as the words were out.

"No, although some of them would be willing to do so, I am sure. Elvenkind do not age as humankind. We continue in good health until we stop. It is our senses that change. As I said, our elders are close to the other side."

"So, what exactly is the prophecy?" Simon asked.

Before Springheart could respond, Madeline heard her name called. Turning, she saw Regis striding towards them. She had to suppress an urge to wave him away. Just when Springheart was about to tell them something, here came his excuse to leave.

As if prompted by her thoughts, Springheart stood. "I must report to my friend on the results of my conversation with the purser. I will contact you soon." He looked at Jode. "Please take care that no harm comes to her while we are apart."

"I do not need reminding that my wife is precious. She is well able to protect herself."

Springheart nodded and then took his jacket, leaving the square as Regis reached their bench.

Regis sat in the place vacated by Springheart. "What an odd person that elf is. I hope that he wasn't leaving on my account."

"I'm sure it was just coincidence," Madeline said. *Just because it happens every time you come around doesn't mean it's not a coincidence.* "It is good to see you again."

"Yes. I have news as well." He tossed his hat onto the table and dragged his fingers through his damp curls. "There are Scree here that we haven't seen before. Not the ones I told you about; these arrived only yesterday."

Madeline glanced at the others hoping they would keep quiet. It would be useful to know if Regis had different information to Springheart. Perhaps something that would convince everyone he was the one they should trust. "Go on. This is very useful."

"The new Scree are young and full of vinegar." He looked at Madeline, and grinned. "I don't think the ambassador will be allowing them to wander the streets. It would not do to have the Scree lose their foothold in The City. They will not do as well if they have to work through an intermediary. And, despite appearances, the Scree enjoy their luxuries."

"What exactly does the Scree ambassador do?" Madeline asked. If ambassador translated correctly, maybe there was hope that they could end this without bloodshed.

Regis picked up his hat to fan himself. "He does what most of the ambassadors do. Buys and sells goods, and information, to the benefit of his people."

Madeline watched Regis' eyes narrow as he spoke, as though he was considering what to say and what to keep close. She decided to share a little of what they knew, perhaps that would help him open up. "Springheart already told us about the young Scree."

"Ah, so I am too late. Well, it seems you know as much as I do." He rose. "I also find myself running a little late."

Madeline shook her head and said, "Please, if you can give a little more time."

He glanced toward the docks, now crowded with people making final deals. The chatter of their bargaining echoing off the buildings. "I can spare a few more minutes."

"Then I will get directly to it. If you remember, I am on a mission to find a mage," Madeline said. "You implied that it was Springheart. Can you tell me more? It seems everyone is either reluctant to speak, or has no information."

The smile that flooded his face reassured her that his ego had overlooked the thickness of the flattery. "I do remember. And yes, I believe that the strongest mage in The City right now is Springheart."

"But surely your powers make you a strong mage," Callisra said.

Madeline mentally groaned. They didn't need to make him suspicious.

He waved a hand to dismiss the thought. "Oh, I am not powerful. My magic is just varied."

"Can you tell us more about Springheart?" Madeline asked.

Regis sat as though he had forgotten the other meeting he had been so anxious to attend. "I do not know much, but I will tell you what I do know. Our elf friend is known in The City, but he has not been here for several years. He returned a few months ago, and has been keeping odd company since he arrived."

Jode leaned closer. "What sort of odd company?"

"Oh, you know. Odd people. Some of them are from the old families, some new. I believe he has been saying that he is here looking for someone important."

"Did you know him before?" Jode asked.

Regis shifted on the chair. "I know many people. But Springheart and I move in very different circles."

Madeline believed him. She couldn't see Springheart being comfortable in the gaming houses where Regis was so at home.

"Do you think he could harm an innocent child?" Madeline hated giving any information on their mission, but being coy wasn't getting them anywhere.

Regis fanned himself again before answering, "If Springheart thought the child was a danger to his own secret quest then, yes. In my opinion he would do whatever it takes."

"I wish we knew more about why he is here," Callisra said. "Are you sure he is on a quest?"

Regis laughed. "You know elves. Either they are on a quest or they are waiting for their own personal prophecy. You can be sure that if an elf is on this side of the elven lands, no matter how little elf blood he has, he is on a quest."

Madeline was getting tired of hints and insinuations. As much as she liked Regis, she couldn't deny that he was almost as hard to pin down as Springheart was. "And do you think you can introduce us to someone who might know something about this quest? Or should we just keep seeking other friends?"

"I will do my best to find someone," he answered. "If I were in need of information about Springheart, I would ask him myself.

His answer may not be the truth, but you would be in a position to decide. And if he chooses not to answer… well that is an answer in itself, yes?"

If I have to do that with everyone in this damn city, Arabela's house will fall no matter how many people come to help. She took a deep breath to clear the anger building. When she was under control, she said, "We owe you a dinner, Regis. Perhaps you can join us this evening and tell us more about yourself."

"I would be delighted. But I have other obligations for the next few evenings. Perhaps I can let you know when I am free."

Madeline nodded. "If we must wait then so be it. When we do meet again, do you think you will know why these new Scree are here?"

"I hope so." He rose and placed his hat firmly on his head. "But I would not concern yourselves overly about the Scree. They would only attack here if they had a very strong reason."

"Would a blood revenge be a strong enough reason?" Madeline watched Regis' reaction. He didn't even pause before answering.

"A blood revenge is rarely served cold. Have you recently done something that would anger a Scree enough to do that?"

Madeline started to answer. Jode touched her knee before saying, "No, not recently."

Regis bowed. "Then, perhaps, it is not the Scree. I will ask my contacts. Now, I really must leave you."

They sat quietly until he left the square.

Jode was the first to speak. "Madeline, I do not like him. Even when he brings us information it is a little too late and not useful."

She felt a wave of weariness wash through her. "I no longer know who to trust and who to suspect beyond just us four."

The evening breeze was rising but all it did was increase Madeline's restlessness. "You're right. We don't know who to trust. So, let's start getting first-hand information. I am more than tired of waiting for everyone to get back to us. Maybe someone can tell us where the embassy is. Come on."

Jode grabbed her arm as she started marching down the street. "Wait. Don't just go barging up to anyone." He waited for her to stop glaring at him. "We cannot storm into an embassy and demand answers. We will need to treat them as though they are a peaceful delegation, no matter what we think."

Madeline sighed. "I am not a child. I wasn't planning to kick down the door and demand answers. I was planning on... Well, I didn't have a plan."

Jode smiled. "I see. Why don't we take a moment to develop one?"

"I've got a better idea," Simon said. "We'll go and find out where to go while you figure out what to do." He took Callisra's hand and led her across the street to a bookseller without waiting for agreement.

Madeline looked around. The street was narrow, so she stepped back to lean against the wall of a shop. Jode lounged beside her. Madeline sighed. She really didn't have a plan, and that bothered her. "What I was thinking is to ask the embassy for some information on their business. No, don't look at me like that. I meant their legitimate business. I thought I could pretend to have connections to help them."

Jode laughed, a loud roar that attracted attention. Madeline shushed him which made him chuckle. "If you don't want me to laugh, you shouldn't say such funny things."

Madeline felt her patience drain away. "I wasn't joking." The irritation built into anger as Jode continued to smile. "If all you're going to do is laugh at me, then go back to the inn." She turned to follow Simon and Callisra into the store.

"No, I am sorry," Jode said grabbing her arm. "Please, come back."

She turned and felt the anger melt. He looked hurt. No not hurt, stricken. It was weird. She couldn't remember feeling this resentment since she'd been in Cartref. Yes, in the old world, it was almost her normal state. But here she spent most of the time happy. Only feeling anger or fear when someone attacked.

"It's okay. I guess I'm just impatient," she said giving him a hug. "I think it's because I was ill this morning. I am afraid that whatever made me throw up will come back. And if it does, I won't be able to save Arabela and Tadric."

Jode squeezed her then held her at arm's length. "You don't have to do it all yourself. In fact, I have an idea."

Before he could explain, Callisra joined them. Simon crossed the street behind her. "The embassies are all a few streets away from The City gate. The shopkeeper said the ambassador is more likely to be there than anywhere else."

Madeline shrugged out of Jode's hands and looked up at him. "What's the plan?"

He painted a look of sympathy on his face. "I thought we might offer our concern that rumors are circulating about an attack."

Madeline smiled at his deviousness. "And give our assurance that we don't believe the Scree are responsible?"

"Brilliant," Simon said. "If we can pull it off, they might let something slip."

Madeline nodded, not feeling overly confident. "I think it would be better if you two waited at the inn. In case... I don't know. Just in case."

Simon looked ready to argue. He had been with her in every adventure so far. But she needed to know someone was going to miss them if something went wrong.

"But," Simon said before Callisra touched his arm.

"No. Madeline is right," she said. "If we all go and the Scree attack, no one will be left to save Arabela and Tadric. And no one will know to come looking for us. By the time Blu realizes we are gone, it will be too late."

Madeline was relieved she didn't have to argue Simon around.

"Thank you, Callisra. If we're not back at the inn by..." She turned to Jode. "What do you think?"

"If we are successful, we may not return until late." He looked toward the city entrance. "If we walk, it's about twenty minutes. We will arrive just before they have dinner."

Madeline's stomach twitched at the thought of food, and she couldn't tell if it was hunger, or more sickness. "Let's just get this over with."

A HALF HOUR LATER, Madeline and Jode stood across the street from a block of offices. The windows were small, with closed shutters. The adobe had been stained a deep blood red. In front of the heavy door stood a Scree guard. He was as tall as Jode, but he was wiry where Jode was solid. The guard's hair was hanging in multiple braids to his ass and he held a spear at his side.

"Not very inviting," Madeline said. "Are you ready?"

"Yes, but remember, they will not want to speak with you. I will do all the talking." He stepped forward. Madeline fell into place behind him as he had explained a woman would be expected to do. It would make things go smoothly. She didn't have to like it. They approached and the guard straightened. It seemed to add four inches to his height. Jode came to a stop and waited. The guard simply glared at them.

"We wish an audience with the ambassador," Jode said after a moment of mutual staring. Madeline had never seen this arrogant side of her husband. She found it kind of sexy.

"I am not his secretary." The guard sneered as he spoke. "Why do you tell me?"

Jode looked the guard from head to toe. "I assumed you had been assigned to protect the house. I see now that you have been made to stand here for the dubious decoration you provide."

What had happened to the diplomatic approach? Madeline didn't speak, trusting Jode to know what he was doing.

"I am only here to deal with possible threats. You do not seem dangerous." The guard stepped aside.

Jode pushed the door open and strode into the hallway. Madeline followed closely trying desperately to ignore the look the guard crawled over her skin.

The interior of the embassy was blessedly cool and dim. Madeline relaxed as they passed through the hallway. At the end, an old Scree woman sat behind something that looked more like a podium, but she treated it as a desk. Madeline saw a grizzled face and shaven head gleaming in the light from an ornate chandelier hanging low above her head. The woman pretended to ignore them. When Jode stopped in front of her, the woman looked up, a question on her face.

"We wish to speak with the ambassador," Jode said.

"You have an appointment?" Her voice was warm and rich.

"No, but we have information that is critical—"

"The ambassador is not available." She opened a leather-bound book and flipped the pages. "You may see him in three days. At ten o'clock."

"Is the ambassador in the office?" Jode asked. Madeline bit her lip in an effort to keep silent.

"In three days," the woman said.

"Make the appointment," Jode said. "I hope for your sake our news will still be of use."

He turned and stalked out of the room. Madeline hurried to keep up with him. When they were safely on the street, and out of earshot, Madeline grabbed Jode and pulled him to a stop. "What was that all about? You were supposed to get us in to see him."

"Short of starting a battle, we were not going to get to see the ambassador. I think that he had given her orders to delay us." Jode looked over his shoulder and took Madeline's arm. "It would be better to leave. I am not convinced that the Scree will simply let us go on about our business."

Madeline felt weariness engulf her. "Fine, but I'm not going back to waiting for someone to tell us what we need." She yawned. "A small snack and a nap, then we're going back out looking for proof that Springheart is attacking." *A good thing that people here stayed out late to enjoy the coolness of the evening.*

"Or Regis," Jode said. "Please, do not forget that he is as likely to be the culprit as Springheart. Or, perhaps, there is another player we don't know about yet."

Madeline felt her anger rising again. Part of her knew it was unreasonable to feel so strongly about someone she barely knew. Well about two someones. But Jode's dislike of Regis pushed her buttons. It was as though he didn't trust her judgment.

"How else am I supposed to figure it out? All we have to go on is feelings because no one will tell us anything," she snapped. "Well that and the vision. If there was another suspect, don't you think Zerenia would have seen something different."

Jode touched her elbow to stop her barreling into a woman with a small child walking toward them on the sidewalk. "You know better than to take a vision at face value," he said, steering her away from the edge of the sidewalk.

"Yes, I do. And I'm not. But Zerenia said she saw Springheart and Regis. That's not open for interpretation. One of them is attacking. I don't know how to tell which one. And that's the problem."

He pointed to remind her that they needed to turn the corner. "Yes, but she said there was also someone interfering with the vision. You seem to think it's one of them. It could have been something, or someone, else. It could be some illness in Zerenia."

Madeline came to a stop and spun to look at Jode. "No. Callisra would have noticed if Zerenia were ill. I hadn't considered someone else as the culprit. Yes. Perhaps the interference came from someone else. Perhaps we don't have to choose between Springheart and Regis."

"It would certainly make life easier. That is if you don't take a shine to the next possibility," Jode said, reached to touch her cheek. "You are very pale. Are you feeling well?"

"I'm just tired," she said. Her stomach growled and she giggled. "Maybe eating will make me less cranky."

"We are almost there." He pointed to the sign hanging outside the inn.

Madeline started walking again. "I guess if there is a third person it would mean we don't need to pick a side. But it wouldn't make life easier. The thing is, we would still have to find this third person."

Jode held the door to the inn open for her. "And we would have to be sure. If we try to find a third person, and it turns out to be Regis or Springheart, I fear we will fail. As you said, we cannot repel these attacks for too long."

Hurrying to the dining room, Madeline said, "I wasn't planning on abandoning them as suspects. I want to stop this even if it turns out to be Regis."

They joined Simon and Callisra in the dining room. The buffet table was filled with small dishes. Madeline noticed some of the delicacies from last night's dinner and felt nausea rise. She filled a plate with cheese, bread, and apples, to be safe.

"Wine?" Callisra asked, holding out the jug.

Madeline wondered why Callisra seemed to be enjoying what she could smell as soured wine from across the table. "I must be fighting a bug," she said. "I think I'll stick with water."

"A bug?" Callisra asked. "Do you think you have been bitten? Should I examine you again?"

It was rare these days for Madeline to use an old-world expression, but when she did, it always made her smile at the oddness of people's slang. "It means my body is trying not to succumb to an illness. Don't worry. I'm sure it will pass. I rarely get sick."

Callisra placed the wine jug on the table and reached for Madeline's forehead. "Let me check your health anyway." She closed her eyes and Madeline felt the warmth of her friend's power flow through her veins. "I only feel tiredness," Callisra said after a moment then returned to her seat.

Simon passed the water jug and said, "Okay, what happened at the Scree Embassy?"

Madeline groaned and let Jode answer. She still needed to take action, but realized that might mean letting the men take the lead, with the Scree, at least.

"So, we just keep hoping they won't attack within The City?" Simon asked. "I guess that will work, but we will have to go home at some point."

"I know," Madeline said with a sigh. "There's nothing we can do about it. I'd rather put my energy to finding Alric's half-brother. When we know that, we'll know who's attacking. And who is helping."

Simon narrowed his eyes and said, "So you've decided to give Springheart a chance? You'll consider that Regis might not be the good guy here?"

She shook her head in frustration. "Am I the only one who thinks that Springheart acts like he's up to something?"

The other three exchanged glances. Madeline picked at her food while they decided who would speak. *Have I been that much of a pain over this?*

"It's not that simple," Callisra finally said. "You aren't usually so set on a course that you can't see the options."

"That's my lawyer training. I used to have to look at all the angles to make sure I represented my client properly." She had represented enough clients that she didn't like. What was it about Regis that made her think he was innocent? "Maybe the longer I'm here, the more I change… No, that's not right." She shook her head. "I'm too tired to work this out."

Callisra rose and felt Madeline's cheek. "You are never so tired either. I still don't feel any sickness, but there is something draining you."

Madeline closed her eyes and tried to sense her own body. Nothing seemed out of place. "I probably didn't get the right kind of sleep last night. Whatever I ate that disagreed with me was probably working its way through my system."

Simon joined Callisra and wrapped his arms around her waist. "You look like you need a nap too. Why don't we all rest. Maybe we'll come up with a plan after that."

"I'm tired of trying to come up with plans," Madeline said. "What were you going to say about how complicated this is? Why you think Regis is behind the attacks."

"That's the thing," Simon said. "We don't have any reason the think it's him. Both of them are acting suspicious. You just seem to be blind to Regis' sneaky behavior. And just as blind to Spring-heart's help."

"Regis is not sneaky," Madeline said. "He's been nothing but helpful. Springheart keeps running away every time Regis appears."

Simon took Callisra's hand and started to leave. Turning, he said, "Regis is always willing to offer help, but he's never actually been any help. He keeps throwing suspicion on Springheart when we push. And you didn't see him at the card table. I can't prove it, but I'm pretty sure he was cheating."

Madeline slumped back in her chair, hunger forgotten. She didn't know about the cheating, but Simon was right about everything else. That didn't mean Regis was attacking the Summer Lands.

She let Jode lead her back to their room. A little voice in her head whispered, it didn't mean he wasn't either.

THE NAP REFRESHED Madeline's energy and her health. The room was stifling. The winds from the ocean weren't getting this far into The City. She needed to get outside soon, but wanted to do something other than wandering around The City hoping for clues. Their only leads were two men, either of which could be the culprit and two old ladies who might or might not have some real information.

She pulled on a light dressing gown then stood in the open French doors staring into their courtyard, thinking while Jode slept. She thought back to when the attacks started, or rather when they realized they were being attacked. Before they set out to rescue Lee. That first attack, when Tadric was so ill so suddenly. Then the sabotage that almost took her life. And, finally, the constant barrage of attacks on Arabela's house. There was no doubt in Madeline's mind that it was all linked, that it would be about who stood to inherit the Summer Lands.

"If only I could contact Blu," she whispered. It would take days for a message to make the round trip on the safe path – days they probably didn't have. If there had been more time, she could have found a way to communicate over the mountains. Time was just something they couldn't waste.

"Come back to bed." Jode's voice drifted to her. "Another half hour and the heat will abate even here."

She turned to look at him, naked under a thin sheet. He was smiling at her in a way that suggested he wasn't talking about sleep.

"You think so?" She drew the curtains over the open doors. It would provide all the privacy they needed.

Jode flipped the sheet off and nodded. "The winds will start again and the temperature will drop."

She grinned and climbed into bed. "I guess we can spare the time to try to make a baby."

THE WINDS DID START AGAIN and the temperature dropped, and more importantly, the humidity eased as the moisture in the air followed the winds out over the ocean.

"Why don't we eat supper in one of the restaurants by the

docks?" Jode said as Madeline returned from her bath. "We could try to contact Regis and ask him to join us."

"A good idea, though I think we should see if there are any Scree about. I don't want them attacking at the worse possible minute. Although, I don't want them attacking at all." She sat at the dressing table and rubbed her hair dry.

Jode took the towel from her and finished drying her hair then picked up her comb. "Can you try to sense them with your magic?"

Leaning back and enjoying the pampering, Madeline said, "I have been thinking of trying to search out clues with magic. I can probably send my senses through most of The City."

He teased at the tangles in her hair. "Could you find Regis and Springheart?"

"Regis would know if I touched him with magic. But, if it was an invitation, it would be okay." She picked through the hairpins on the dresser and found two silver ones. Passing them to Jode she continued, "I don't know about Springheart. Do you think he would be offended if I reached out?"

"I have no idea. Now, your hair is done, do you need anything else?" Jode sat on the bed and took her hands. "You look better, thank goodness. Are you feeling better?"

Madeline nodded. "Just make sure I don't fall off the chair while I'm casting."

She closed her eyes and sent her senses out through The City.

It was quiet. She could sense people moving around outside the inn. She sent a request through her powers. *Regis, we invite you to meet us at the docks when you are finished with your business.*

She expected her power to leap for him, but it simply continued to float through The City like fog. She sensed the shopkeepers opening their doors for the evening traffic. If Regis wasn't available, perhaps Springheart would be. Madeline sent the request out. *Springheart, are you there?*

Still no response. She sighed and cleared her thoughts. If

neither of them were near enough to feel her call, she would test for threats in the area. She tried to push her power faster through the surrounding streets, but it was like pushing water. It flowed at its own pace. She tried to grasp it, pull it together, but it just slipped away.

Madeline tested the intent of every person she could sense as her magic flowed. There were small twinges of greed and betrayal. She recognized the stealth of a thief a few streets from the inn. A child cried in a nightmare. A woman glowed with love.

A sour feeling lurked at the edge of her senses. There was hatred there. Still unable to exert any control over her powers, Madeline had to wait for it to flow around the threat. The sourness increased and she felt her stomach turn. It was strong, but she couldn't tell if it was coming from one very angry person or from a cluster of people. The only certainty she had was that the hatred was directed at her and it chilled her to her marrow.

Madeline tried to focus in deeper, but she still couldn't get a grip on the flow of power. Suddenly the hatred twisted, the taste going from sour, to bitter, to foul as though someone had flushed a sewer through her mind. She recoiled and felt her body respond.

She opened her eyes to see Jode reaching for her from above. The sense of her body returned, and she realized she was lying on the floor.

"Madeline, I am sorry. It was so sudden." He lifted her and put her on the bed. "You were fine, as you often are with your magic, relaxed and calm." He kissed her forehead. "Then you threw yourself backwards. I tried to catch you but—"

She pulled him closer. "I'm fine. Don't worry." As she said it, the memory of the fetid stench of hate rolled back to her. She pushed Jode away and ran for the bathroom.

7

*R*eturning to the room, Madeline mopped her face. "I sorry, that was a really bad session."

Jode helped her back to the bed. "I've asked Callisra to come. This time, please let her examine you."

Madeline squirmed herself into an upright position, back against the headboard. "Okay, but I think it was just the vision. There was a horrible stench. I'm sure that's what turned my stomach. I don't feel ill."

"It would make me feel better to know." He kissed her forehead. "I would not want to lose you because we didn't take a moment to heal whatever this is."

Madeline nodded, pushing away the fear that she truly was ill and didn't know it. She felt healthy enough to keep pursuing the clues. But if this sickness was just the start of something more serious, she might be laid up for days. And in those days, the attacks could break through the protections around the house.

"Madeline," Callisra's voice broke through her spiral of worry. "I need you to open your mind to me."

"I'm not blocking you." Madeline tested her defenses and

found a swirling wall of protection. "Oh, I didn't realize I was doing that."

Callisra smiled before closing her eyes, and then placing her hands on Madeline's forehead and chest. Madeline felt the probing of healing magic and relaxed into the warmth of it. Just being in contact with the healing power drove away the lingering nausea.

"Hmm. I sense an imbalance, but not sickness," Callisra said as she settled in the chair beside the bed. "Jode said you were searching for the sense of danger? Tell me exactly what happened."

Madeline summarized her experience. "The closer I got, the worse the smell got. I think it was just that."

"How are you feeling now?" Callisra moved to the curtains and opened them to let in the breeze.

"Better." Madeline stretched and felt the tightness of her shoulders and back release with the effort. "In fact, much better than I have for a couple of days. Thanks, I hope you didn't give up too much energy for me."

Callisra shook her head. "Very little."

"So, this imbalance, what do you think it might be?" Madeline mentally crossed her fingers.

"It could be the heat, the unfamiliar food. Perhaps it's the stress of our mission and the fact we are making little or no progress." Callisra studied her hands for a few moments. "I don't like not knowing, Madeline. Are you sure nothing else is wrong?"

Madeline thought about the way her magic seemed to defy her but decided to keep it to herself. "No, nothing. So, if I am not ill, there's no reason we can't get back on the streets looking for clues." Madeline slid off the bed and started for the door. "Come on. We always get something at the docks. Let's go back there now. I get the feeling that people will be more chatty at the end of the day. And I'm more than ready for dinner."

"If you still have your appetite, there can't be much wrong. Just try to stick to plain food." Callisra opened the door to her room while Madeline waited. "It looks like both of our husbands are ahead of us."

When they entered the lobby, Jode's face lit up. Madeline hurried to assure him she was fine. "Callisra didn't find anything wrong, so you can stop worrying, my love." Jode looked over her shoulder at Callisra, confirming the diagnosis. "Hey, don't you believe me?"

He kissed her again before saying, "I would not put it past you to understate bad news until we have found our attacker."

Madeline couldn't deny his accusation, but she thought she'd been better at hiding that stubborn part of her. "Well, now you have the confirmation that I'm not going to collapse, let's get down to the docks."

"I sent a message to Regis to meet us for dinner at the Wild Buck restaurant," Simon said, returning his attention to the group after checking on Callisra.

"If you know where he is, couldn't we just go meet him?" Irritation flooded Madeline's mind and she tried to control her reaction. "As much as I like wandering around, it would be much better if we could just get on with it."

"I don't know where he is," Simon answered. "But it occurred to me that he's pretty well known in some quarters. I paid a couple of the servants here to look for Regis and invite him. We might get lucky. If not, it was only a few pennies. And don't forget he already said he has business to attend to."

"Sorry, I don't know why I said it that way. It was a good idea. Maybe we should do the same with Springheart." As she said it, Madeline wondered if they could get the two men to sit still together long enough for a meal.

"Perhaps not tonight," Jode said. "I don't think that we will get any information out of either of them if they are together. It will just be a competition of who can find an excuse to leave first."

Madeline laughed. "You know it might just be fun to try to make them stay. But let's concentrate on one of them at a time."

As they walked to the docks, Madeline noticed the way the streetlights glowed in overlapping circles of warm yellow light along the street. It gave a feeling of safety despite the darkness. "I noticed these lights the other day. Are they lit with gas?"

Jode followed her glance. "They are made from the Ettran stones."

Simon and Madeline exchanged glances. "What are those?" Madeline asked when Jode didn't seem to think the statement needed further explanation.

"Of course, I forget sometimes that you don't know all that I do. Ettran stones are a local phenomenon. You will have noticed in other places; the darkness is illuminated with torches. In Arabela's home, they use candles in special holders."

Madeline nodded.

"Here there is a quarry that yields Ettran stones. They glow at night as long as they are exposed to light during the day."

"Like solar panels," Simon said. "Why don't they export them? It's got to be much safer than burning torches."

"The stones are difficult to transport, and I suppose no one has seen the need to replace the torches with something that might shatter in transit." Jode turned to say more, but suddenly went still.

Madeline reached for her knives as she whipped around to face whatever threat Jode had seen. There was nothing behind them. Relaxing she turned back Jode. "What did you see?"

Jode was still alert, but his sword rested in its sheath. "A Scree. He was following us."

"How far back?" Madeline stepped forward as though it would make a difference to what she could see. "Where is he?"

"He turned and ran when I saw him," Jode said taking her arm. "He was very young. Not that it makes a difference, Scree are dangerous as soon as they are able to stumble from their mother's side."

Madeline stared into the shadows between the streetlights. "Only one? Should we go back?"

"No. Look. The restaurant is only a few doors away. We are safe for now. I am told that the Scree will not attack where there are witnesses. On our return, we will need to be cautious."

Madeline paused long enough to send her magic out as far as her eyes could reach. There was no sense of danger, but then, there was no sense of anything.

When they arrived at the restaurant, they were seated at a table in the far corner. Madeline chose a chair that allowed her to watch the entrance. She wanted to see Regis arrive, if he decided to join them, afraid that he would turn and leave at the last moment.

"We may have another guest," Callisra told the waiter. "Perhaps we can start with some wine and a plate of those."

Madeline turned to see Callisra pointing to a table covered with more of the local delicacies. Her stomach twitched at the sight. "Water for me, and if we can have some bread and cheese as well, that would be fine for now."

"When I said plain food, I didn't mean you had to eat like a monk," Callisra said. "I'm sure a glass of wine would not hurt you."

Madeline didn't want to tell Callisra that the odor rising from the wine was like drain cleaner. "I think it's best to be safe, especially with the possibility of Scree jumping us on the way back. Don't worry. I'm not planning to deprive myself of that great looking stew." She nodded toward a table where a family shared a platter of meat and vegetables that looked so savory it made her mouth water.

"It is called a hunter hash," Regis said as he slipped into the chair across from her. "I am so happy that my plans changed. It is wonderful to see you all again."

"It is good to see you again," Madeline said, annoyed that she'd missed him entering. Jode responded with a little nod in Regis' direction. Madeline wanted to kick him. If her husband couldn't be pleasant, it was going to make it difficult to find out what Regis knew.

The waiter returned with the wine and appetizers. Regis praised their choices and offered to order the meal. "You must try the specialties of the house." He turned to the waiter without giving anyone a chance to speak. "We will eat family style. Please, tell the chef to send his favorite dishes, and, another bottle of this fine vintage."

The waiter nodded and headed to the kitchen.

"Now," he continued. "You must tell me how your search for this mage is going. I have made little progress, but it may help to combine our knowledge."

Madeline let the others bring Regis up to date and studied his reactions, trying to find any evidence of his innocence, or guilt. He listened to the little information they gave with nothing but an expression of interest on his face, as if they were telling him the latest gossip.

If she thought she could get away with it, Madeline would have sent a probe to test the truth of his reactions. But he would sense it just like last time. And that could end any chance of getting what they needed.

Jode finished with their experience at the Scree embassy.

Regis shuddered. "The Scree are truly uncivilized when it comes to their women. They keep the women for breeding more soldiers, you see. Now they cannot see any reason that women would be able to do more than that."

Madeline remembered a few men she'd known, back before she came here, who would make perfect Scree. "We can handle the Scree, I think," she said. "But tell us what you have found out, Regis. We cannot allow this mage to continue his actions much longer."

The waiter approached, so Regis waited until the food was placed on the table. "Thank you, this looks perfect," he said. "Now I must insist you each take a sample of the dishes before we return to the intrigue of the hidden mage."

Gritting her teeth, Madeline realized that Jode was right. Regis was a master at diverting the conversation away when it came to real information. Was that because he had nothing to tell her and was embarrassed, or because he was a poor liar, so he avoided anything other than the truth. At second consideration, he was too good at cards to be a poor liar. "It is vital that we find this mage," she said as she placed a spoonful of rice and fish on her plate.

"A few more minutes will not make that much of a difference, surely." Regis passed her a chunk of the bread that came with the meal.

Madeline tasted the food without arguing, not sure if it was because she knew pushing wouldn't speed up the process, or because her hunger rushed back at the flavor of shrimp, and butter, and rice filling her mouth. She glanced at the others and realized they were waiting for her to take the lead. Looking at her plate, she filled her spoon again. If Regis thought he was in control of the pace of news, she needed to take it back. When she finished tasting the crisp vegetables, Madeline tried to match his tone, light and teasing. "I am more curious about your news than I am hungry. After all, we are strangers here and you know so many people. We are at your mercy."

She saw pleasure cross his face. At least she'd flattered his ego. Now, if he would just give them something, she could go back to liking him, and stop imagining his every move and word were hiding lies.

"I could be of so much more help if I knew the exact problem," he said.

Madeline felt an impulse to tell him everything, just checking her tongue in time.

"I regret we are not at liberty to tell you," Jode said before she could speak. "It is a matter of delicacy. Not our secret to share. I'm sure you understand that."

As Regis flicked a glance at Jode, Madeline saw something raw in his eyes; pain, or anger, or perhaps fear, then it was gone.

"Yes, secrets are dangerous things to share," Regis said quietly. A smile replaced the expression and he waved his hand in dismissal of the serious atmosphere. "I have little more to give you. You know that Maltius is rumored to have fathered a child, but I have not been able to find out more about the mother. I have confirmed that there are only four people in The City who are strong enough to be called mages."

Madeline waited, but Regis seemed willing to keep the drama high. He passed a platter of meat to Callisra and poured more wine in the four glasses.

Just as she was going to ask, he seemed to remember they were waiting for him to tell. "Ah, well one of them is Lady Madeline and I assume that she is not who you seek." He laughed, but when no one joined in, he became serious. "The other is Zerenia. She has a reputation for secrecy and no one is sure of her allegiances, but you are looking for a man, I believe. Springheart is possessed of strong magic, and I am also considered talented. I hope you trust me."

So, no information we didn't have before. Madeline found herself starting to agree with Jode. If Blu trusted Zerenia, then she wouldn't believe Regis' insinuations. "What is Springheart's magic?" she asked.

"Like all elves, he is able to use herbs to create potions, but our Springheart is also able to send his magic to distant places."

"How?" Madeline thought of the attacks. Could it be something other than the magic humans cast from their minds?

"I understand he will create a potion and then somehow cause it to act elsewhere." He looked at the ceiling. Finding inspiration there, he continued, "Most elves create a potion and then sprinkle or pour it onto the subject. Springheart has found a way to create a potion that will float in the air and follow the winds to a subject in the distance. I apologize. I have no details. But it is well known."

THE DINNER ENDED EARLY, Regis leaving just before the bill arrived. Madeline was not ready to settle in for the night. "I think I've had too many naps. I feel like I could stay up all night," she said, turning to Jode. "It's so quiet. If we keep an eye out for Scree, we could walk around and get an idea of The City without the crowds."

Callisra covered a yawn. "I am feeling the weight of the day and the meal. Simon, would you mind if we had an early night?"

Simon grinned and agreed. "If you don't need us..." he raised an eyebrow. Madeline looked to Jode, not willing to take the responsibility of splitting their party.

Jode winked and said, "I think we can manage to protect ourselves." The two newlyweds slipped away to the street leading to the inn.

Jode took her arm and started walking. "Why don't we walk to the other end of the docks and see what is down some of those streets. We haven't explored enough of The City. Perhaps if we seek new areas, we will find more information?"

"Yes. Maybe we've been focused on the easy places." She swept her arm around the broad walkway. "It should be safe here, don't you think? No one will be able to sneak up on us. And the Scree magic only works in close quarters."

Jode looked around and nodded. "Unless our mystery man attacks us, we should be able to relax." He hugged her close. "I was worried about you this afternoon."

"I'm fine now," she said, giving his arm a squeeze. "Callisra must have been right about the food."

"I hope so." He kissed the top of her head.

"What you just said, about the attacker turning on us, I hadn't thought of that." She shrugged a shiver off her shoulders. "The attacker knows why we are here, if it is Springheart or Regis, they would be watching for us to make the connection. If they thought we were getting close, they could turn the attacks on us."

"Yes, "Jode said. "And they have a ready-made scapegoat in the Scree."

Madeline didn't want to consider any further complications. The lapping of the water was calming and made the empty dock feel less lonely. She took Jode's hand and they walked in silence toward the last street leaving the dock. Looking down it, Madeline saw the familiar sight of bars and small merchants, all closed. The establishments changed to residences before the street curved away toward the city wall.

"This doesn't look promising. Let's try back the way we came." She turned and caught the sound of a guitar and drums. "Wait, isn't that one of Simon's songs?"

"Yes. I've noticed that some of our music has made its way into the bars of The City. Simon seems to be happy with the situation."

"Yes, he really does want to change the music here." She pulled Jode towards the source of the sound. Just around the bend of the road, a cheerily lit pub beckoned, its door wide open, bright light flooding the street in front. "Let's see what else they can play. We'll be safe in there."

They found a perch on stools near the door. Madeline asked Jode to order a beer for her. She could almost taste the hops in her mind. While he was gone to the bar, she looked around at the crowd. Most were watching the two musicians, both goblins, beside the bar. But there was a buzz of conversation and bursts of laughter as well as music to fill her head. It was a welcome distraction from the idea that Regis might have lied about everything. She had a growing desire to test Jode's theory by bringing the situation to a head. It would take some talking, but she should be able to do it.

Jode returned with Springheart in tow. "It seems we've stumbled on a very popular place."

Springheart bowed and for the first time, Madeline saw a smile cross his face. It took years off him. Then she remembered he'd mentioned the Scree as well, unless he was colluding with Regis, who he clearly detested, the Scree were probably actually attacking her. It felt reassuring to have something settled.

Springheart leaned in to speak in her ear over the music. "Lady Madeline, your husband tells me that Simon was responsible for this new entertainment."

She nodded. Trying to stop herself drawing back. Reminding herself that he had done nothing to justify her fear. The song ended and the duo announced a break. After a smattering of applause, and a few catcalls, they stepped through a curtain to the back. The noise level dropped enough to allow them to talk without straining.

"We have missed you," Madeline said. "I hope you can stay a little while this time. You are always so busy rushing off here and there."

Madeline ignored Jode's raised eyebrow. If a little coquettishness would get him to talk, she'd flirt with Springheart all night.

"I am able to stay and share a drink." Springheart smiled again as he spoke. "But, yes, I am the first of my clan to visit The City in many years, even though there are a few more elves here these days. Along with my quest, I carry a list of errands almost as tall as I am."

"Do the elves not trade here on a regular basis?" Madeline asked.

"Yes, but not my clan. My mother was here as a young woman and since then, only a few have come."

Jode turned from watching the crowd. "And you have only

come because of this quest. Do you still believe that Madeline is who you seek?"

He nodded. "I do. We know that the person has great magic, but very few other clues were made available to me."

Seeing an opening, Madeline said, "We were told today that there are only a few people with strong magic in The City."

"Yes," Springheart said. After a pause, he added, "Only four including me."

"I wish we could be of more help to you. Can you tell us what clues you have?" Madeline asked.

"The answers will not be clear, but I believe I can say that the person I seek is not only powerful, but is capable of more than they know, and has a secret. But this does not help. What have you learned about your own quest?"

"I believe we are seeking one of the four mages. Perhaps it is the same person you are seeking." Madeline felt a touch of the itch that came when her magic awoke. "Perhaps we will find a mutual solution." The itch faded away. She knew there was something important she was missing, but it was gone.

Springheart stared at her. "I sense you are looking for someone who is working against you. That you are here to stop them. I do not believe we are looking for the same thing."

Madeline tried for a casual tone. "Do you have a guess at who we might be looking for?"

"I would not plant accusations without proof," Springheart said. "I believe we are both in the same position. We are only sure who it cannot be – ourselves."

At least Regis is trying to help. Springheart just adds more complexity. "It seems we are both stuck until we have more information."

"I do have something to tell you. If you recall, I offered to find out something about the Scree?"

Jode turned back to the conversation at his words. "Yes, we

have seen a Scree youth. And we tried to talk to the ambassador, with no success."

Springheart nodded. "It seems the ambassador is unavailable to anyone. My contact in the service hall at the embassy thinks he has left The City."

"If the ambassador is not there to control the younger Scree…" Jode tensed and took a step closer to Madeline.

"Yes," Springheart finished his statement. "There may be less desire to abide by the laws. I advise you to always carry arms."

---

8

*M*adeline woke the next morning and waited to see how she felt; no dizziness, no nausea. She'd slept well and, other than the lingering feeling that she should know what to do about Regis and Springheart, she felt well.

Rolling over, she noticed that Jode was gone. She stretched and then started getting ready for the day. The French doors were open to the courtyard, but the air was still and the room felt stuffy already. That didn't bode well for the day. She dressed. A glance through the curtains, and she realized why the morning breezes were absent; it was already afternoon.

She rushed to the dining room to find Jode sitting with Callisra and Simon; they were drinking tea. "Why didn't you wake me?" she asked as she joined them.

Jode kissed her cheek. "You were deeply asleep, and I thought you would benefit more from the rest than we would gain in continuing to wander the streets of The City looking for clues."

Callisra looked at her. "Are you feeling well?"

Madeline nodded. "I'm fine. I just need to eat. But what are we doing today? Or what's left of the day."

Jode's answer was cut off by the entrance of one of the maids.

"Two messages came for you, Lady Madeline." She passed a sealed roll of paper and a cream envelope with red borders to Madeline. Looking at the sideboard, she said, "You have missed both meals. I will ask the cook to make up a small plate for you."

Madeline started to say not to bother she'd find a restaurant when her stomach growled. "Thank you, but just something simple. Is Zerenia taking visitors?"

The maid looked over her shoulder before answering. "No. My mistress has left The City. She will be back in a few days."

Madeline's skin itched with warning. She hoped that the innkeeper had her own business out of town and the warning wasn't danger for Zerenia. "I guess we're not getting any news from her today either."

Jode poured tea and passed it to her. "Here, perhaps this will help your mood."

"I'm not in a mood. You should have woken me. It feels like we've lost a whole day."

Callisra reached for Madeline's hand. "This is not like you."

Madeline pulled her hand away. "I'm just hungry. I'll be fine as soon as I've got some food in me."

She tamped down the irritation and opened the scroll. Her mood lifted immediately. "It's from Blu." She held it up to read the contents. "It's not much. The attacks are continuing, but they are now confined to the night. I wonder if that's because the attacker is tiring too. I hadn't considered that might happen." She rerolled the message and placed it on the table. "He has no information for us, but asks that we hurry. The defenders are tiring."

Jode took her hand and gave it a squeeze. "Don't get discouraged. We are going as fast as we can. It will be different when we have some clue to point us in one direction and not every direction. We have connected with the two people who are most likely to be the culprit. Once we know which it is, we will end the attacks quickly."

The cook passed her a plate of bread and stew. "I am sorry it is not something finer," he said.

Madeline remembered the effect of the last fine food. "It is perfect. Thank you, I'm sorry to be a trouble."

He muttered a dismissal of her concern and returned to the kitchen.

"What about the other message?" Simon asked, pointing to the small envelope.

Madeline took a mouthful of the stew to quiet her appetite before breaking the wax seal. Chewing, she read the cream-colored card inside. "We have been invited to supper."

Callisra raised an eyebrow. "Do we have time to socialize?"

"Oh, I think this is more than socializing," Madeline said, waving the card. "Our friends from the park have issued the invitation. I have a feeling we are going to get some gossip that we can use. I'll send our acceptance. At least it feels like we are going to get somewhere today."

THEIR AFTERNOON WAS NOT FRUITFUL. The spice merchant had no further information. No Scree jumped out to be dealt with. And neither Springheart nor Regis was about. They bought a small hostess gift of candy to take that evening and returned to the room to get ready.

The doorman at the inn had arranged for transportation and now they stood in the lobby of the Gorelle's home.

"Oh, don't you look lovely, ladies," Olieva said hustling them through the door. "And you gentlemen, so handsome. Come. Eilein and cousin Viette are waiting in the drawing room. We'll have a few little drinks before dinner. I am so looking forward to the delightful evening."

They followed Olieva into a lavish room filled with brightly upholstered chairs and small ornate tables. Everything was colored in vivid blue and yellow. In the far corner, the other two ladies were sipping something that sparkled in finely etched glasses. Both smiled and beckoned.

"Good, now we can pour your drinks," Viette said. "You know it's not a good idea to pour elven wine more than a minute before drinking. Oh. You might not know that. Have you ever tasted elven wine before?"

"No, I haven't," Madeline said, taking the offered glass. She sipped and felt the tingle of bubbles run through her body. "It's delicious," she said, and then placed her hand over the top of the glass. "No more. I need to keep my wits about me."

The women giggled. "Oh yes, if you drink more than one glass you will definitely lose your wits. If you enjoy this, then you must come to the Magister's ball this weekend," Olieva said. "I heard a rumor they have the latest vintage."

Madeline sipped the wine and said, "If we are free, I would love to, but we have to locate someone."

"I am sure you will find out what you need," Eilein said. "It is as important to enjoy yourself as it is to fulfill your destiny, Madeline."

"Unfortunately, our mission is vital," Madeline answered.

The ladies ignored her words and started chattering about the latest fashions, and a party they were hoping to be invited to on the following weekend.

Realizing the futility of pressing, Madeline spent most of the hour biting back her urge to interrogate them about Springheart. She would just have to let them take their time, but her initial certainty that they would get information was still there.

Despite the warning about losing her wits, Viette reached for a third bottle of the wine, only stopping as a chime rang through the conversation. She clapped her hands. "Dinner is ready. I do hope you have brought your appetites. Our cook is well known for her creativity. Come."

She took Madeline's arm and led her into a sumptuous dining

room. The table was covered with plates decorated in intricate patterns of deep green and black. The multitude of cutlery arranged at each setting looked like it was solid gold.

Olieva sat at the head of the table with her sister and cousin sitting between each of the couples. She nodded at the servant and a clear soup was placed in front of each diner. Madeline took a careful sip and tasted vegetables and shrimp. "Wonderful. I've never tasted anything like this."

Olieva simpered. "Yes, I told you she was talented. This will prepare your taste for the next course."

"I cannot wait any longer to tell them," Viette said. "We have found some information for you."

Madeline waited while the soup was replaced with a rice dish that was barely a spoonful. If all the servings were this tiny, she would be hungry when they were finished. "I'm happy to hear that. We have not been so successful ourselves."

"We asked our neighbor if he remembered Maltius," Olieva said, gesturing for them to eat. "He did! They were great friends."

Madeline tasted creamy pepper in the rice. She nodded to Olieva to continue.

"Well, it turns out that there were children. Two boys. Isn't that exciting?" Olieva giggled.

"It is," Madeline said, hoping there was more information. "And their mothers?"

Olieva winked at Madeline, an oddness that seemed to fit with the whole character of the evening. "Well both women returned to their families before giving birth. Maltius did not know the children existed, we are sure of that. Our neighbor kept in contact, but neither family wanted their shame to be known. I think it is more likely that neither wanted to release the child to the Summer Lands."

"Now here is the interesting part," Viette took over the conversation as the rice was removed and replaced with a fish stuffed with herbs. "It seems that our neighbor saw both boys in town this week. We think that he meant Regis and Springheart. What do you think of that?"

Madeline swallowed a morsel of the fish, spicy and rich. "We suspected this might be true," she said.

"Well, what you may not know is that both of them have a shady past," Olieva said gleefully. "Neither did we, I assure you."

Madeline put her fork on the plate and waited for more information.

"I can see you did not know," Viette said. "Aren't we clever to have found that out?"

"Yes, you have been very helpful. Is it possible for us to speak to your neighbor?"

Olieva gestured for the servant to bring the next course before answering. "He has left The City for his annual retreat. I don't expect him to return for several weeks. Now, try this dessert. I have not finished telling you what we learned."

Madeline looked in the pastry bowl that the maid placed in front of her; there was a murky sauce with black seeds scattered across the top. She looked at Jode, then Callisra, they were grinning widely. Simon was looking at her with an expression mirroring her own feelings. How could this slimy looking mess be dessert?

Jode laughed. "Try it. I promise you have never tasted anything like it. My mother used to make this for me. Not many cooks will bother these days."

Madeline dipped her spoon in the mess and then touched it to her tongue. A burst of citrus filled her mouth, then cinnamon, and a final aftertaste of dark chocolate. "Oh, it is… I don't know a word to describe it. Thank you."

The women all laughed at Madeline's reaction. Olieva spoke, "It is a good luck sweet. It takes three days to prepare. I am honored that you like it."

"Do you know what this shady past is?" Jode asked, letting Madeline finish her dessert.

"I have no real details," Olieva said, suddenly serious. "My neighbor either didn't have the information or chose to be discreet. But I can guess at least about Regis."

"Gambling debts," Viette blurted. "He is a scoundrel. The rumor is that he had to flee the Downs because of his gambling."

"And he is unrepentant," Eilein announced. "A real scoundrel."

Madeline picked up the last fragment of pastry. "And Springheart? Do you have anything you suspect?" She popped the pastry in her mouth.

"Elves are very secretive," Olieva said, shaking her head. "I have only heard that there is a rift between him and his family. But that must be something very bad. Elves hold family sacred."

AFTER DINNER, Olieva offered the household driver to take them back to the inn. "I will sleep better if I know you arrived home safely," she said.

The carriage dropped them off at the front door and Madeline waved the driver away before turning to Jode. "I'm not ready to go back to the room. Can we go for a walk?"

"Not us," Callisra said. "We are looking forward to our beds." She led Simon through the inn door with a cheerful laugh.

Jode looked Madeline over before saying, "If you are sure. Are you armed?"

Madeline smiled and patted her bodice where her throwing knives were concealed. "I have been ever since we saw the Scree." She looked at his evening clothes, snug fitting trousers, short boots, and a white shirt under a leather vest. "I can't believe you have a sword tucked in there somewhere."

He lifted his hand and flexed his thumb. A knife slid into his grip. Then he bent and drew a matching one from his left boot.

"A sword is not the only weapon I am familiar with. Let us walk, then. But not too far, I don't like being on the streets at night."

Madeline blew out a breath in frustration. "It's fine. Everyone says that the Scree will keep the peace." He gave her a stern look. She rolled her eyes. "Fine, put away one of those and I'll take out one of mine. I want to hold your hand like we did when we were first married." *When things were peaceful.*

He slid the knife back into the arm sheath and waited until she had the haft of a throwing knife in her hand before putting his free arm around her shoulders. "Let's head toward the docks. It seems likely to be busy, and I will feel safer in a crowd. And we know the territory; a little familiarity is what we need."

Madeline snuggled into his shoulder and sighed. "Let's talk about what we are going to do after this."

"It will be nice to contemplate a time when we are not searching for an attacker, or hiding from an attack. We talked about staying here for a while. Do you still like that idea?"

Madeline shook her head. "I think I will have seen enough of this city before we are done. But a holiday sounds like a good idea. Are there ships that take people as well as cargo?"

"A tour of the coastal towns?" He looked down at her. "I do not know if living on a cramped boat for days is my idea of a holiday."

She remembered her thought as they rode after the Choi. Was that only a few weeks ago? "What about camping? I would love to take some time to explore the lands we keep rushing through."

"You would be happy sleeping under the stars? Hunting our food?" He gave her shoulders a gentle squeeze. "It bears some thought. Perhaps you and I could travel back to the Summer Lands along the coast. Simon and Callisra must want some time to start their marriage."

They reached the docks before Madeline could answer. The normally bustling space was deserted. A few streets away, the glow of light from the two or three still open bars, was the only competition for the moon when they stepped from the street onto the loading area. The sounds of laughter and music carried across the open cobbles and water. "It's so peaceful," she said moving to the center of the space. "You can hear the water lapping. And that faint song. Can you hear it, Jode?"

He joined her and drew her to him. "It is as though we are the only people here. It has been a long time since we were alone. I had forgotten how much I enjoy it."

"If I close my eyes, it's like I can hear the echoes of the day. Like the commerce soaked into the stones of the dock and the buildings." She allowed Jode to wrap her in his arms. "Now I can hear your heart. And the wind – what was that?"

Jode spun her and faced the sound that had shattered the moment. An arrow vibrated from where it had struck a bollard. "Run." He pushed her toward their street.

Madeline ran, pulling Jode along with her. A howl came from the darkness of an alley. Then two more arrows flew, striking the cobbles only inches from Jode's heels.

"Scree," he hissed. "They think no one will see if they attack here."

Madeline skidded to a stop as a Scree youth blocked her path. He grinned at her and yipped a command. She glanced to where the arrow had come from. Two more Scree rushed from the shadows.

"Madeline," Jode said as he turned to protect her back. "Show no mercy. They will not stop until we are dead, or they are."

She flicked her knife ready to throw and slid a second one from her skirt. "Knives won't go as far as arrows."

She felt Jode jerk his arm to release his second knife. "They have discarded their bows. They want this to be personal."

Madeline stopped listening to anything other than the sound of breathing. Jode's was ragged and she felt herself gulping for air. She stared at the eyes of the single Scree blocking their escape. He grinned and licked his lips. Then, as he flicked a glance at his companions, Madeline threw her knife. It buried itself into his chest, but on the wrong side for his heart.

She felt Jode lunge toward the Scree behind as she rushed to finish the job. Her victim was still stunned with surprise. She took advantage of that and slashed at his throat. He recovered enough to drive his own knife into her arm, but too late. Madeline's blade had severed his carotid artery. He fell back as the blood arced from his body. She reached to grab the haft of her first knife, pulling it loose as the body fell away.

Spinning, she saw Jode had already dispatched one opponent and was struggling with the second. The hilt of a knife stuck out from Jode's shoulder. Madeline felt the world shrink to the combat in front of her. Her own wound forgotten, she lunged forward, knife held like a spear in front of her.

The Scree was slicing the air in front of Jode, and her husband was managing to deflect the attack. But he was weakening. Madeline grabbed Jode's hand. Pulling him out of the way, as she ducked under the arm of the Scree and stabbed upward, embedding her blade in his heart. He collapsed on her. As she lost consciousness, Madeline heard footsteps and shouts approaching.

"MADAM, MADAM" Madeline surfaced to the male voice. Two men came into focus as she blinked her eyes open. They were looking down at her and their facial tattoos matched, causing her to wonder if she was seeing double for a moment. Hands reached to help as she struggled against pain and dizziness to sit. Someone had tied a bandage around her arm. The pressure of the wrapping only increased the throbbing. As soon as she was upright, Madeline twisted looking for Jode. "Where is my husband? He was hurt. Is he… is he…"

"He is fine," the man on her right, answered. "Look." He pointed to where Jode was standing, speaking to a third man with the same tattoos. "As soon as he knew you were going to survive, he made his report."

"Report?" Madeline tried to think through the fog that threatened to push her back into unconsciousness.

"Yes," the second man said. "I am Orman. That is Xiana and that is Nomenta." He pointed to each of the other guards as he named them. Nomenta, the other man who had helped her, was running toward a side street. "We are the watch for this area. We saw the Scree in hunting mode and ran to see what we could do to stop whatever they were planning, but arrived too late to intervene."

Madeline shook her head to clear the thoughts and regretted it as the scene spun around her. "Please, help me up. I need to speak to my husband."

A firm hand pressed her shoulder from behind. "I'm right here. Please, Madeline, lay back down until we can get Callisra. I've asked one of the watch to bring her. You have been seriously wounded."

Madeline lay back on the cushion of a cloak that someone had folded behind her head. "The Scree attacked us. We only defended ourselves," she said to the waiting Mariai.

"Yes, we know," Orman said. "We saw enough to know you did not start this."

"What will happen? To the Scree?" Madeline noticed the three dead bodies were piled together. As much as she knew they had no choice, it still tore at her heart to see lives ended so easily.

Orman glanced at the corpses. "We will burn the bodies as is their custom. The ambassador will pay a fine, and have to face some repercussions. But you do not have to concern yourselves about that."

Madeline opened her mouth to ask if the repercussions would stop future attacks, but a glance from Jode made her close it.

"Let me pass." Callisra's voice was strained with worry.

Madeline started to sit only to fall back as pain lanced

through her arm. She closed her eyes and waited until she felt Callisra sit beside her. Blinking her eyes open again, Madeline saw Simon rush past to join Jode who was speaking to the watchmen.

"Let me see that arm," Callisra said, her voice gentle.

Madeline felt Callisra's touch and then warmth flowed through the wound. "Don't wear yourself out," she whispered as the pain receded. "I need you to take care of Jode, too."

"Do you think he would allow me attend to him and let you wait? Let me make sure you are in no danger of dying, and then I will go to him." Callisra looked at the wound and nodded. "This will finish healing by itself. Any other symptoms?"

Madeline sat up to test the dizziness. The world stayed on a normal axis. She touched the wound that now looked like a scratch. "No, I'm fine. Please, go and check Jode. He was stabbed and now he's pretending nothing is wrong."

Callisra took Madeline's chin and looked into her eyes. "I sense something, but it's not serious. Stop fretting. I'll make sure Jode is healed."

Madeline struggled to her feet with Orman's help. She stood and watched as Callisra tested Jode's shoulder. The healer said something that made him grimace and then slowly raise the arm. Callisra placed her hand on the spreading blood, and Madeline saw a rich orange glow cover the wound. Jode sighed in relief as the glow faded.

When the healing was done, Jode shook the Mariai's hand and made his way to her side. "The watch is satisfied, at least as satisfied as I can make them. They always have more questions than anyone wishes to answer. Let's get back to the inn. If I know anything about healing, Callisra will be falling asleep in a few minutes and I don't know if I have the strength to carry her."

"Don't worry. She's my wife. I can carry her." Simon looked at Callisra and continued, "Well, maybe we can get the watch to help."

Callisra gave him a playful slap. "That's the problem with marrying a musician, all talk and no follow through. I will be fine."

Simon pointed to the street. "Okay go ahead. I'll watch your backs. There's no guarantee that the Scree are finished with us."

9

*T*hey settled in Simon and Callisra's room with mugs of tea. Callisra curled up on the bed, her eyes already drooping. She yawned and muttered, "Are you feeling okay, Madeline? Jode?"

"Go to sleep," Madeline said. "We'll be fine. I promise we won't undo your healing."

"Perhaps we should talk in our room? Let Callisra sleep in peace," Jode offered.

Simon looked at his wife who was already snoring gently. "No. I would rather we stayed here and made sure she rests properly."

"So, not to state the obvious, but the Scree seem to have decided they don't need to worry about the city rules." Madeline rubbed her arm as she spoke. The wound was tender, but nothing like the dizzying pain earlier.

Jode settled his hip on the edge of the dresser before speaking. "I wonder if the ambassador's absence is the reason they felt free to attack. They were all young. Tempers run strong at that age even in humans."

"So, if the ambassador returns, the Scree will go underground again?" Simon asked. "And we won't have to worry about them until we leave? That's hard to believe."

Madeline agreed with Simon, things with the Scree were getting out of control. Not that control and Scree were words that fit together well at the best of times. "It might be worth trying to talk to the ambassador again." She held up her hand as Jode shook his head. "I mean, you. I get that they won't want to talk to me. I'm just a woman after all."

"Is there any way you can tell with magic where the ambassador is?" Simon tucked the sheet over Callisra's legs, then looked over his shoulder at Madeline. "I mean, can we be sure that he's out of the city? If he's just avoiding you, that's different from actually being unavailable."

Madeline thought about the last time she tried to search for someone with her magic. She hoped that had been an anomaly. "I'd need to know way more about him, and the embassy, to scry. I think I can send a thread of magic through the building and sense the occupants. If I sense him there, that should be enough, right?"

"If you are sure," Jode said. He put his tea on the dresser and reached for Madeline's hand. "I do not want you to overtax yourself." He patted her hand as she opened her mouth to argue. "I know. I know, you feel fine, but you have not been well. I do not want to see you ill."

Madeline leaned in to kiss his cheek. "It won't take a lot of energy. I promise I will take care. If anything feels wrong, I will pull out." She settled herself in the only chair in the room. "Okay, let's get started. How will I know I've found the ambassador?"

Jode rubbed his head in thought. "He will be the oldest Scree male in the house. I heard something about him being injured. It was why he became ambassador, no longer able to fight." He closed his eyes and was silent for a minute as he dug for the memory. "Yes, he lost three fingers off his right hand. Can't hold a sword."

Madeline nodded and prepared herself. Starting with blocking all distractions by visualizing her beach. The image of warm sand and the gentle lapping of waves calmed her enough to start the search. She felt her power rise and flow from her body. Forming it into a probe, she shot it out to the city.

At the door to the embassy, Madeline felt the presence of a guard, perhaps a different one than they saw. A slight resistance slowed the probe. Madeline added a pulse of energy and it slipped inside. She waited, trying to sense whether anyone was near the lobby, but no life energy pushed back.

She took a deep breath and prepared to slip through the building, thinking about how she would work her way after leaving the reception area. She pushed at the thread of power and it resisted. Madeline tried to sense what the barrier was. Had she tripped an alarm? Was there someone in the way?

Suddenly her power whipped back to her. Gasping at the snap of pain as the probe rocked her, she tried to force it back to the embassy. Her power curled into her gut and settled. She grabbed for it, but it slipped through her control again. Fear leached the heat from her body and Madeline sucked in a deep breath. If she couldn't control her magic, she would be useless.

She tried to return to her beach, to center herself before panic swept away her emotional control. She managed to restore the sensation of warmth and felt a second of comfort before she felt hands grab her.

"Madeline, please answer me," Jode's anguish tightened his voice.

She opened her eyes to see his face, pale and frightened. "What happened?" She struggled to sit up from her slump in the chair.

Simon handed Madeline a shawl, and she realized she was shivering. "You just went limp," he said. "It took us five minutes to revive you."

Panic threatened to drive her back into unconsciousness. She couldn't tell them that she had lost the only thing that made her valuable. "I couldn't get into the embassy. It's nothing. I guess the wound took more from me than I thought. I'll be fine in the morning." She stood and took Jode's arm. "Let's go back to our room and rest."

"No, I know you better than that." Simon stood. "There's something else. You need to tell us what happened."

"What do you mean?" Jode looked at Simon then turned to Madeline, eyes narrowed. "What happened?"

Madeline looked at Callisra who was sleeping deeply. They wouldn't disturb her unless they got loud. And it didn't feel like any of them had the energy for loud. Knowing neither Jode nor Simon would let her wiggle out of telling something, she gave up and told them what happened. Blurting it out before she could stop herself. "It's like I didn't have any control of my magic."

"Do you think someone was using a counter spell?" Simon asked. "Like you'd tripped an alarm?"

"I didn't sense anyone else involved," she said. "Usually I am in total control of the magic. Like it doesn't exist until I call on it, but this time the magic just took control." She held up her hand at Jode's alarmed face. "No, not of me, but control of itself."

"I don't like this at all," Jode said. "First you are ill and now your magic is misbehaving. If Blu were here, you'd ask him for help."

Madeline nodded feeling tears of frustration rising unexpectedly. She took a breath and calmed herself before speaking again. "Maybe Callisra will know something after she's rested. Maybe… Maybe it will just fix itself like the sickness."

Simon moved closer to Callisra. "I hope she'll be rested enough. I worry about her stretching herself too far." He stroked her cheek. "She has been our only healer for too long."

The tears started to rise again and Madeline swallowed, trying to keep them from falling. "Look we're all getting maudlin. Callisra is going to be fine. My magic is going to be fine. We'll figure out who is attacking and stop them." She clenched her fists as though she could make the words true by sheer effort.

Jode looked like he was going to argue but gave his head a small shake before speaking. "Until we can ask Callisra to assess your health, perhaps we can talk about our other problem. I have been thinking about these attacks. Whoever is doing this must have a motive."

"Yes. They want to take the Summer Lands from Arabela and Tadric," Madeline said. "We know that. Do we have to hash this out again?"

Jode shook his head. "Yes, I think it will help to talk about it. It's not good strategy to simply pick a reason and blindly go after it. That's why I think we've forgotten to ask if there is other motivation."

Madeline was relieved to change the topic from her magic, but wondered where Jode was going with this new direction. The events of the night were catching up with her and she was looking forward to her own bed. They would never make headway if they drove themselves to exhaustion. "You think we've decided on who the attacker is, and only looked for motivation to prove it?"

"Perhaps," he answered. Then, looking around, he seemed to notice how worn out everyone was. "I am sorry. You are normally so strong. I forget that you are not trained to quickly recover from a fight. Let's continue this conversation in the morning."

"No, finish your thought," Simon said. "I think we can all last a few minutes longer. And I'm not sure any of us will sleep with this in our minds unfinished."

"If we think the motive is that one of Maltius' bastards is trying to overthrow Arabela, then we must believe it is Regis." He waited as though expecting Madeline to argue, but she nodded for him to finish his thought. "I cannot see any resemblance in Springheart to Maltius or Alaric. In fact, as much as I try, I don't see anything but elf looking back at me. Regis on the other hand has a familiarity about him. Nothing I can point to, but a gesture, or expression that recalls Alaric."

"That neighbor of the Gorelle's said there were two of Maltius' sons in town. Do you think the other is a stranger?"

"Unless we can speak to this man, we cannot know if he is reliable. He is away from The City for some time. I hope that we are finished with this before he returns, but should every other lead take us nowhere, we could search him out."

"I hope it doesn't come to that. So, if we look further for motive?" Madeline asked, still not willing to accept that Regis was the villain. "What other motive is there?"

"It is unusual for Scree to be anonymous in their attacks, but these Scree are unusual. They attack in The City, and they seem to be bent on a revenge that the other Scree have set aside."

"You think the Scree are trying to finish what Sayer started?" Madeline wondered why it hadn't occurred to her. "What about Zerenia's vision?"

"Could the Scree have sent something to interfere?" Simon asked. "If the thing that held her in place and caused the flickering was something interfering and not part of the vision..."

"How will we find out?" Madeline rested her chin on her hands. "Do you think Zerenia would know? We can ask in the morning if she's back."

Jode rose and reached to take Madeline's hand. "Perhaps she can also learn something about this problem with your magic? Come. I think it is time to find our rest."

Madeline let him lead her out of the room, saying good night to Simon as the door shut behind her.

Slipping between the covers only minutes later, Madeline said, "If Zerenia isn't back tomorrow, maybe we should send a message to Blu by land. I know it will take days, but the only other people here who might be able to tell me what's happening to my magic are Springheart and Regis."

He drew her into a hug. "If it comes to it, would you ask?"

She considered. She was worried enough to need an answer, but could she trust anyone? "If it gets worse, or if Zerenia isn't back in a couple of days, I will ask Springheart."

Jode drew back to look at her. "Are you coming to believe Regis is our attacker?"

She chuckled. "Maybe, but Springheart seems more serious and knowledgeable. I'm not sure Regis has the attention span for studying, so his answer may not be reliable."

"Well, I see that as progress." He kissed the top of her head. "A good night's sleep and we'll have fresh perspective in the morning. I will return to the Scree embassy after breakfast. Perhaps I can get some information by threatening a scandal over the attack."

Half asleep, Madeline murmured something encouraging and snuggled deeper in his arms.

—————

*T*he next morning Madeline woke feeling strong. Jode was still sleeping beside her so she slipped quietly from the bed to get ready for the day. Within ten minutes, she was leaving the room in search of Zerenia.

Madeline stopped the first maid she saw in the dim hall. "Is your mistress at home?"

The girl smiled and glanced into the breakfast room. "She is, Lady. You will find her supervising the cook's assistant in there."

Hunger squeezed her stomach at the sight of the food being arranged for the buffet. Madeline stopped to fill a plate before accepting Zerenia's quiet invitation to join her.

"Have you made any progress in your quest?" Zerenia asked.

Madeline poured more tea for her hostess before filling her own cup. "It doesn't feel like it. I guess we've stirred something up because we were attacked last night."

"How terrible," Zerenia said. She glanced at Madeline checking her out from toe to head. "You seem to have survived."

Madeline nodded, and gave Zerenia a summary of the events. "So we are still stuck in the same place, looking for clues about

Regis and Springheart. But now we might have to add the Scree to the mix."

"I do not think the Scree are involved in the attacks on the Summer Lands." Zerenia waved her hand as though to clear smoke away from between them. "I mean to say, not in my vision. I know when the Scree, in fact, I know when any creature enters my vision. The confusion was part of the vision not interference."

Madeline nibbled on a slice of toast while she thought. "Is there a way you can go looking for another vision?"

Zerenia laughed. "It is not like shopping for a dress. You do not keep trying visions on until you get one you like."

Madeline sighed. "I need to get this stopped. Blu says the defenses will not last forever. Do you have any suggestions? Or could you scry Blu?"

"The conditions will not be right for that kind of magic for a month or more." Zerenia settled back in her chair. "I have been wondering why you do not set a trap. Your sole approach is to ask questions. As if someone is going to tell you who the attacker is."

Madeline stifled her reaction, thinking that Zerenia didn't mean to belittle their investigation. Maybe Jode had been right last night. Maybe they had gotten blinkered. Not about the two possible culprits, but about what to do. "Setting a trap requires bait. I don't know if I have enough information to put out the right bait."

Before Zerenia answered she gestured for someone behind Madeline to join them. Jode pulled out a chair and accepted a cup of the strong tea.

"Simon tells me that Callisra needs more rest." He shook his head at Madeline's worried look. "She is going to be fine. I told them to stay and refresh their energy. We may need her skills as healer again before this is over."

Madeline told Jode what Zerenia had suggested. "It is time to make a change," he said. "But you are right. What would we bait the trap with?"

"I am not sure whether to be happy that there are people so inexperienced in subterfuge, or shocked at your naivety." Zerenia pushed her empty plate toward a maid who was checking the tables nearby. "Lili, take this to the kitchen."

When the maid had left the room, Zerenia continued, "She is a new member of my staff and I am not yet sure of her loyalty. I think it would be better that your plans are kept secret for now."

"I appreciate that. But there's another question," Madeline said. "Even if we bait a trap, how will we get either of them to it?"

Zerenia leaned close. "I have an answer for both of your questions. What did you do with the message from Blu?"

"I still have it," Madeline said digging into her pocket. "Here. I've been keeping it with me."

Zerenia smiled. "This is good. Now, no one has seen the contents other than you and your friends?" Jode shook his head. "Then, you can claim it contains any information you wish, and that will be your bait." Zerenia waited and Madeline was reminded of her law professor. He would expect his students to put things together.

Madeline's brain seemed to be having difficulty following the thread as fast as she usually could. "You mean…" She sighed and started again. "If we let people know it came from Blu, and the contents were enough to tempt…" She felt something click. "Yes. We could say that Blu was bringing Arabela and Tadric here, or taking them somewhere safer. If that rumor got to Regis and Springheart… No, if the rumor said there was a message about Tadric, and someone was willing to sell the information…"

Zerenia clapped her hands quietly, glee showing in her eyes. "You are devious. I knew it."

"I was a lawyer in the past," Madeline said with a snort of laughter. "I have spent the last year trying to suppress everything about that. I'm glad it has finally come in handy."

Jode raised his cup in salute. "How will we get this rumor started and aimed at our two mages?"

Zerenia stood and said, "That is where we use the loyalty of my staff. Leave it with me. Be ready to go in a few hours." She left them as other guests started to drift into the room.

"Feels like progress," Madeline said. "I'm starving, but that won't fill a few hours. What could we do to amuse ourselves?"

"I have a few ideas." Jode raised an eyebrow. "But you will need your strength, so go and fill your plate."

MADELINE SAT at the table in the small lobby later in the day waiting for news. For something that meant they could get back into action. Jode's ideas for distraction were more than pleasant, but even he couldn't keep lovemaking going on for hours. The rest of the day had been spent gossiping and playing cards with Callisra and Simon. Going out and searching again didn't seem like a good idea while Zerenia spread rumors about the letter. She knew the logic behind staying in, but Madeline was bursting to get the plan underway. It had been a week since they had decided to come here. As far as she was concerned, that was five days longer than it should have taken to stop the attacks.

Zerenia walked into the lobby with one of the young kitchen boys at her side. Madeline watched as she bent to whisper something that sent him scurrying to the street. Zerenia joined Madeline in the corner where three comfortable chairs were arranged around a tiny table. She glanced around before speaking, "The rumors have been going out for two hours. I have made sure that Regis and Springheart will hear no matter where they are."

"So, we just need to get to the meeting place and see who shows up?" Simon asked from his place by the desk. "What exactly was the rumor?"

Zerenia smiled. "It has been too long since I was involved in such subterfuge. I had so much fun developing the message. I must find a way to do this more often. Anyway, the rumor said that the contents of Blu's message were for sale. That was Manal, the boy I just sent. He will be the one who sells your letter. I think it is more likely a servant would do this thing, do you agree? This way you will only need to observe and apprehend."

Madeline itched to go after the boy. "It seems a good plan. Where are we to go?"

"I thought the docks would give you the best chance to catch whoever comes to the meeting. It is customary for people to meet there and conduct, shall we say unorthodox, business. When you come to the end of this street, turn to the left and stay in the shadows of the stores building. Do you remember where that is?"

Madeline nodded. "I think that's where the Scree hid out last night. It's the one with a row of windows near the roof."

Madeline noticed Jode glance at the street before he turned back to the discussion. "Should we contact the watch? If we are going to apprehend someone, then we need a place to keep whoever comes to the meeting."

Zerenia shook her head. "If you contact the watch, someone may... no, someone will, let slip that it's a trap. And they are not interested in a problem that affects the Summer Lands. They will only act if the city peace is disturbed."

Madeline itched to finish the quest. It seemed so close. "When should we go? The docks won't be in shadow until nightfall. If we go now, we will be seen."

Zerenia rose before speaking. "An hour is all you will need. The stores building will close soon. You may want to change into darker clothes and then make your way to the rendezvous."

"Supposing this works, where should we take the person?" Callisra asked before Madeline could voice the question. "We will need to talk to them somewhere."

Zerenia glanced toward her own door. "I have made arrangements. Bring him here. You will have all the privacy you need."

. . .

AFTER CHANGING into dark tunics and trousers, Madeline and her party headed for the docks. The streets were still bustling with people, but they were mostly headed back into The City, to their homes, or places of business.

Madeline burned to run to the stores building but knew it was no use. Arriving sooner would only mean a longer wait. She must have been hurrying anyway since Jode felt the need to take her elbow and gently slow her pace. "We stand out enough in these clothes, Madeline," he whispered. "Don't bring more attention to us."

She sighed and slowed down. "If we are too late, the deal might be done. I don't want to leave Manal in danger."

Jode squeezed her arm. "That is admirable, but the boy will not know if we are there. He will simply exchange the information for the money and leave. Now, do you have any other reasons to rush?"

Madeline chuckled and nudged Jode. "I was hoping to finish this tonight and get on with our lives."

He kissed the top of her head and directed her around the corner. "We are here. Perhaps you will get your wish."

They walked the last few feet towards the stores building. Madeline scanned the docks. They were deserted, but she could hear the faint sounds of activity from further along. People were enjoying dinner and would be out soon to wander between restaurant and pub, looking for entertainment.

"Look, there's Manal," Callisra said. "I hope we won't have to wait too long for Regis or Springheart to show up."

Madeline didn't care which of them came, just that someone would. It was long past time to finish this off. As she watched, Manal turned and took a step toward the glow of the streetlights nearest their hiding place. She looked deeper and saw a flash of long braids and a click of bones. Scree!

Jode grabbed her arm as she moved to defend against whatever attack was coming. "Don't move," he whispered. "They are leaving. We are not in danger. Look at the boy."

Madeline glanced back at Manal who had returned to his place. "When this is done, we'll deal with the Scree. I am not going to be looking over my shoulder for the rest of my life."

Jode smiled. "Yes. I am looking forward to dealing with that problem as well. Now watch."

"Hush," Simon hissed. "Look it's time."

Madeline snapped her attention back to Manal, still standing alone. Then she scanned across the expanse of paving and saw someone stumble out of a side street. He was dressed in plain gray from head to toe, his face covered with the hood of his cloak. By the build, it could have been either Springheart or Regis. Whoever it was had been in a fight. Leaning forward she tried to make out what was said. Manal turned slightly so that the man limping toward him would face the watchers. "You have the message?" The voice was weak and Madeline could barely tell it was male. The fight must have damaged his throat.

"You have the money?" Manal asked. "I was told you would have money."

The man nodded and drew a purse from under his cloak. "Five hundred. I have protected this with my life. This message had better be genuine."

Madeline watched as they exchanged the bag for a folded slip of paper. Manal ran from the docks as soon as he had the purse. She noticed he chose a street other than the one leading to the inn. The man was struggling to open the folded paper. Madeline could see his hands were bloodied, and at least two fingers were bent in a way to suggest they were broken.

Not willing to wait any longer, Madeline rushed out of the shadows. She heard the others follow and so did the man who still had not opened the letter. He turned to see who was rushing him, his hand slipping to where his sword would normally be.

Madeline continued to run reaching out to pull the hood from his face. Before she touched it, he reached up and lowered it himself. Regis.

She stopped suddenly. The feeling of betrayal so strong she almost cried. "You!" She managed to choke out. "You have been attacking the Summer Lands? You have been trying to kill Tadric? He's a child. He's your nephew."

Regis twisted his mouth into a grimace. "They did not care to bring me into the family. Why should I care that the boy is Alric's spawn?"

Madeline's stomach twisted. She had defended him, and he was just as everyone warned her, worse. Her hand clenched into a fist that she raised to punch the smirk off his face. Then she stopped. He was unarmed. He was badly injured. And it wasn't her place to punish him. Arabela would want that privilege. She kept her eyes on Regis as she said, "Callisra, can you tell if he is well enough to come back with us? Or will you have to heal him here?"

Before she went to Regis, Callisra touched Madeline. "You are trembling. Go walk off the stress while I check him. Right now, he is too injured to do any harm to anyone. I will be safe."

Madeline felt the adrenaline burn through her veins. As she moved to obey, the trembling turned to dizziness followed by a wave of nausea. She ran to the edge of the docks and emptied her stomach into the sea.

Jode reached her just as she finished and brushed her hair off her forehead. "Let me bring Callisra. Regis can wait."

"No," Madeline said, the sourness in her mouth matching the bitter feeling of betrayal. "I'm fine. It was just a reaction to the shock. I'm not ill. I'm fine."

He looked at her as though he was going to argue, but simply kissed her forehead and drew her back to where Simon was holding Regis' arms while Callisra ran her fingers over the man's chest.

Callisra looked up as they approached. "He will survive the trip. I don't like to move him in that state, but it will be safer to deal with the healing in private."

Madeline looked at Regis. He was paler than usual, but there was some fire left in his eyes. She couldn't wait until they got back to the inn to get answers. "Why? Why did you start this?"

"No one cared about my mother. Maltius disappeared and left my mother to face her shame." His voice was weak, but the hatred shone through.

Madeline knelt at his side. "I don't think that's what happened. I don't think he knew."

Regis glared at her. "I know what I know. Now, let us go so that you can do what you need to do."

"Can you walk?" Madeline asked. The docks would soon become busy as the last diners came looking for more interesting places to spend their evening. Madeline had no desire to attract attention.

Regis grunted and tried to shake Simon off. "I can as long as it's not too far."

"No," Jode commanded as Simon released Regis. "Keep him restrained. We will walk him to the room. I do not trust him."

Despite his assurances he could manage by himself, Regis was sagging between Simon and Jode's hands as they walked across the docks. Madeline wondered if he was trying to slow them down for some reason. But a second glance at his face, gray and sweaty with pain, changed her mind.

They were halfway to the privacy and safety of Zerenia's room when Madeline heard running. She turned, hands reaching for her knives, to see Springheart approaching. "I heard there was another attack," he called. "Are you hurt, Lady Madeline?"

Madeline waved the others on and waited for Springheart to reach her. "No, this time the Scree attacked Regis." It occurred to her as she spoke that they didn't know why Regis had been the target.

Springheart leaned to see around her and voiced her question. "I wonder what he has done to attract the attention of the Scree. Attract it enough to have them break the peace two nights in a row." He brought his attention back to Madeline. "I heard about the incident last night. You look fit. Your healer is very skilled."

He said the right words, but Madeline didn't sense any real feeling behind them. She didn't know enough about elves to know if it was normal, so she put the thought aside until she could ask Jode. "Yes, she is. Were you looking for us?"

He checked over his shoulder. "Yes. But if the Scree are still out, perhaps we should go somewhere safer. They may not be finished with Regis of the Downs yet."

"We are taking him to Zerenia," Madeline said. "Why don't you join us? It will give us a place to talk."

*a*s soon as Regis was installed in a small chamber behind Zerenia's private sitting room, Callisra healed his wounds enough to ensure he would live. They left him sleeping and bound to the bed to meet in the empty guest dining room.

"He will sleep for an hour or so," Callisra said. "I healed him enough that his own energy could finish the task, but that is all. I don't think we want him up and running around."

Madeline was taken aback. She had thought healers would have taken a similar oath here. "Is that ethical?"

Callisra shook her head. "No. I didn't mean that I was keeping him weak. I meant I didn't drain myself to heal him. He will gain back full strength in a couple of days."

"Good," Madeline said, relieved. She turned to Springheart. "Our quest seems to be over."

He glanced at the door before answering. "As is mine, but before I speak of that, please tell me about these attacks."

Jode leaned forward. "Why do you want to know?"

Madeline observed Springheart and let Jode control the conversation. She didn't think the elf had anything to do with the attacks on Arabela, at least she no longer thought it, but she didn't trust him. He was hiding something. It might be benign, but it might not. Springheart paused long enough that she thought he might be constructing an answer. She reached for her magic to try to probe him, but it still evaded her grasp. Annoyed, she simply watched as he thought about what to say.

Springheart finally flicked his fingers as if he was dismissing a troubling thought. "When I heard you were attacked, I thought I might be able to assist in resolving it. But now they have attacked Regis, I am not sure. It seems more complicated than I first thought," Springheart said. "Perhaps if I have more information I can still help."

Madeline lifted her eyes from Springheart and noticed that everyone seemed to be waiting for her to answer or respond in some way. She looked again at the elf, wishing she could sense him with her magic, but it wasn't responding. Nothing was going as planned. She wanted to take Regis and go back to Arabela's. Then she would know that everyone was safe. "Before we tell you anything, what can you do to help?"

He smiled. Such a rare occurrence that Madeline was shocked at the change. His face opened up and he seemed years younger. "I have some favors owed to me. I had hoped to trade those to the Scree and ask them to put aside whatever they were pursuing against you."

Madeline told him the details of her history with the Scree. "You know that the Scree are seeking blood revenge on me."

"Yes, but I do not understand why they attacked Regis of the Downs. Do you have a theory on that?" Springheart asked.

"We will ask him when he wakes," Simon answered. "I do not like my wife putting herself out for someone who would attack a defenseless child." Callisra patted Simon's arm, but didn't contradict him. Madeline noticed her friend was pale, and wondered how much energy she'd had to give to save Regis' life.

"I think it is time for some trust between us," Springheart said. "I apologize for being so reticent up to now."

"I think that's a good idea," Madeline said. "Why don't you tell us about your quest?"

"Mistress," the doorman spoke before Springheart could start explaining. "A messenger has arrived. He wishes to speak with you."

Madeline looked over the man's shoulder to the street door. *What now? Couldn't things wait for an hour? For the time it would take for Springheart to finally tell us what he's up to?* "Where is he?"

His eyes widened in surprise, or fear. "It is a Scree, mistress. I didn't wish to let him in until I knew you would accept him."

Madeline looked at the men around her. "I think we have sufficient protection here. It is only one Scree, isn't it?"

The doorman smiled. "Yes, but sometimes that is sufficient. I will show him in."

Springheart shifted in his seat slightly, catching Madeline's attention. She saw him slide his sword from its sheath. Glancing at Jode, she saw a blade appear in his hand too. Nodding she armed herself. "Simon, Callisra, go to your room. If this goes wrong, we'll need you to be ready to help."

Simon hesitated for a second and then led Callisra away. They passed a young Scree who strode into the dining room without acknowledging them. His braids, hanging to his hips, rattled as he walked. Madeline looked closer and thought she saw finger bones twisted in with the shells and feathers.

The Scree stood a good six foot four and was only a teenager by his unlined face. He ran his eyes over the three people waiting for him to speak. Madeline didn't need her magic to see that a sneer was only barely kept off his face.

"You may place your weapons back in their holders," he said. "I am not here to do battle. I am here to present the ambassador's invitation. He has expressed his hope that it might bring an end to the conflict."

Madeline slid her knife back into the hidden pocket but didn't look to see whether Jode or Springheart did the same. "Your people have attacked me and my husband. And tonight, you attacked Regis of the Downs. Why should we entertain anything you say? If the ambassador wants the conflict ended, then he can just end it."

The boy worked his jaw as though he needed to spit out a foul taste. He looked at the two men and frowned when they didn't rescue him from having to converse with a woman. "The first attack was a mistake." The Scree glanced down as he spoke. Then he seemed to gather himself and continued, "The ambassador will explain the second attack. He believes that we can end this problem between your house and the Scree."

Madeline wondered if the Scree were all in agreement. It didn't matter, if there was a chance to stop one set of attacks, it would be worth the risk. "Well then, what is this message?"

Swallowing first, he glanced one more time at the men. When they didn't speak, he looked at Madeline and let the sneer crawl across his lips. "You have been summoned... invited to the embassy in one hour."

Madeline toyed with the idea of not going, but only for a moment. If it were a trick, they'd find a way to deal with it. "We will be there."

The Scree twisted his lips. Madeline told herself it was a smile. "The invitation was only for you."

"We will be there. My husband and Springheart will join me." She held the boy's gaze and he was the first to look away. A trickle of pleasure at his discomfort ran through Madeline's body.

He tensed and then nodded once. "I will inform the ambassador. It is his decision to allow you to bring your companions. I have delivered my message. You are invited alone." The Scree spun on his heels and strode out of the room.

When they were alone, Madeline sighed out her tension. "Do you think it's legitimate?"

Jode put his sword on the table and rolled his shoulders. "I do not trust the Scree, but I think we have no choice."

Madeline turned to look at Springheart. Things had shifted since the Scree entered and the elf had willingly pulled his weapon to defend her. She found her suspicion of him had melted away. "And what do you think?"

"I agree with your husband. I find it hard to trust the word of a Scree, but they have offered to end this feud. It seems to be worth considering, don't you think?" He raised his eyebrow.

She nodded. "If they do mean to end it, then I'm happy to meet with the ambassador. Have you heard about them brokering a peace in the past?"

Springheart gave a little shrug. "With the Scree, it is sometimes hard to know what will happen."

"Do you think I should go alone?" Madeline felt magic flush her skin, but couldn't decipher the message. Was it telling her to go alone, or to take her two companions?

"No," Jode said before anyone else could speak. "I do not care what the ambassador wants. I am not letting you go there alone."

Springheart touched his sword. "Jode is correct. We must go with you. I have some skills when it comes to negotiation. If that fails, I am also quite good with my sword."

A door opened and closed in the back of the building, the flash of light from the room reflecting on the mirrors. A second later Simon stepped into the room. "I see everyone is in one piece, so no need of Callisra's skills."

"No. So far we're fine. She must be tired anyway." Madeline offered him a glass of wine. "Should we check on Regis?"

He declined the wine with a wave of his hand. "I'll go. Callisra said he'd be out for hours and it's been less than one."

Madeline stood and stretched the tension out of her body. "We have been invited to the Scree embassy to resolve our differences."

Simon's face brightened. "When do we leave?"

Madeline heard something crack in her spine and sighed with the release of tension. "You and Callisra stay here. If Regis wakes up before we get back, you can try to get some information out of him. Now we've got him, I have no idea what to do next."

Simon started toward the door. "Unless you are going to be gone until morning, he won't be telling us anything. Callisra said he would be too weak to do more than sleep for at least a day. I should come. The more swords on your side the better."

And leave this inn unprotected? Madeline wondered where the thought came from. It had no taste of magic, but she couldn't ignore it. "I would feel better if you were to stay here."

Simon frowned and then seemed to accept her request. "Stay safe, then. I don't want to have to tell Callisra that anything happened to you. Or Arabela for that matter. Try not to start an all-out war."

Madeline laughed. "You give me too much credit."

"While we're waiting," Madeline said to Springheart, "why don't you tell us about your quest. Is it over? Have you found the person you were seeking?"

Springheart nodded. "I believe so, at least the first part. I am certain that I have found the woman I seek. Before I tell you the details of my quest, I would know if you trust me."

Madeline felt a blush heat her cheeks. She knew that he deserved better than she'd been thinking, but keeping Tadric safe was more important than worrying about a stranger's feelings. "I believe people earn trust, Springheart. I had no reason to trust you when we first met."

He nodded slowly before answering. "But I do not know what I did to have you instantly suspect me. You did not feel the same about Regis."

Jode moved closer, to protect her, or stop her digging herself in deeper, Madeline wasn't sure. He said, "It was important that we—"

Madeline touched his arm before interrupting, "No, he is

right. I seemed to give Regis more benefit of the doubt than he deserved. Jode, you were quick enough to argue about it, don't feel you have to defend me." She turned back to Springheart. His face showed no blame or accusation. "I don't know why I felt as I did. I'm not usually so easily influenced."

"And now, do I have your trust?"

Sensing the importance of his question in the intensity of his gaze, Madeline answered with complete honesty. "I have no reason to distrust you, but I have no reason to fully trust you. Every time we come close, you leave for some reason."

Springheart dropped his gaze to look at a scroll he held in his hands. Considering for a few minutes — minutes that Madeline thought they didn't have — he finally looked up and said, "It is vital to the success of my quest that we have trust between us. It is true, I cannot expect you to follow blindly, given your recent betrayal by Regis. I cannot give you details until we have established that trust. But I see the impatience on your face. We have no time to discuss this now. Let us deal with the Scree and perhaps then we will have the time to come to an agreement."

Madeline wanted to say she trusted him if only to stop him stalling, but knew he needed it to be more than just words. She tried to send a finger of her magic to touch Springheart, but it wouldn't respond. *Another thing to deal with when this night is over.* "Let's go and see if we can tie up one more of the threads getting in our way," she said.

12

When they arrived at the Scree embassy, the guard reached to open the door without comment. A Scree woman met them halfway down the hallway and led them to a small room tucked behind the reception desk. There were three chairs facing a large desk, no chair on the other side.

"If they are expecting this to intimidate us, it's not working," Madeline said, pushing away the twinge of fear that sprang from somewhere inside.

"Patience, my love, this may not be a test of your courage, just a way to minimize our access to the embassy."

"I think it's more likely a test." Madeline glanced around the room. "I don't see any peepholes. If they aren't watching us, why leave us here."

Springheart gestured with his hand as if painting a line around the room. When he finished, he said, "I sense no watchers, real or magical. Why do you not send your magic out to seek presences?"

Madeline considered giving Springheart an excuse but realized that lying would not help built trust. If he were going to be an ally, she would have to start trusting him, or at least act as if she did. "My magic is not functioning properly."

Springheart leaned closer to look in her eyes. His hand on her shoulder felt comforting. Madeline felt the probe slide behind her barriers, but it came with a sense of protection. Something within her reached out to meet the probe.

"I apologize. I should have asked permission," Springheart said pulling the magic probe back.

Madeline reached for Jode's hand, wanting contact before she asked, "Did you find something?"

Before he could answer, three Scree marched into the room and lined up facing the seated group. "Lady Madeline," the oldest Scree said. "You are here to answer for the death of Meesela of Goddard's tribe."

Madeline noticed the lack of fingers on his hand. Standing, she drew on her lawyer attitude. "I would like to speak to my accusers." She heard Jode and Springheart rise to stand on either side of her.

The ambassador gave a short nod to the Scree at his right, and they left. "You will meet them soon. First, we wish to acknowledge the attack on you was not sanctioned."

"That is good to know, but I would think you had better control over your people." Madeline stared at the ambassador. Tall and lean, he looked like a thirty-year-old badly disguised as a seventy-year-old. The vitality of the younger man shining through the wizened features of the elder.

The smile that flowed across his face was genuine. Madeline hoped she had scored some points.

He laughed. "A woman with spirit. It is unusual to see that in this building. Perhaps that will be to your advantage."

"What does she need an advantage for?" Jode asked.

"The honor duel," the ambassador's tone was surprised, as though it was obvious why they were here. "She must settle the debt with her life, or she must end the line of Meesela's family.

Now, even though she is merely a woman, in this case she will speak for herself."

Madeline placed a hand on Jode's arm to reassure him and gave a silent thanks that Springheart was keeping quiet. "Why now? It has been more than a year."

"It has taken some time for the family to gather and track you." He glanced over her shoulder. Madeline turned to see the Scree messenger had returned and was standing beside the ambassador. She realized that the noise they had made marching into the room earlier was a deliberate intent to intimidate. They could move silently when they wanted.

The messenger nodded to the ambassador and turned away.

Madeline turned back to face the old Scree. "Why are you answering my questions? I thought you didn't acknowledge women."

"You have impressed me. And you are about to face death. It would be impolite to refuse information to someone who will be dead in a very short time. If in the unlikely event that you are not dead, you will have earned the right to any knowledge you desire."

Madeline wondered what information she would need from the Scree. "When I asked you why now, I meant why this particular time. Why not tomorrow?"

"Tonight, we removed your distracting mission. We damaged the man who is attacking the Summer Lands. Now you can concentrate on the duel. Your friend will be safe and when you are killed, these two can deal with Regis of the Downs. It is the perfect time." The ambassador smiled as though his speech was cause for celebration.

Madeline felt the weight of lost time drain her. "You knew who was attacking the Summer Lands? How?"

"I assumed that the bastard side of the family would attempt a coup," the ambassador said. "It is what we would do."

"How did you know that Regis was Maltius' child?" *If the Scree knew this, who else might have known? Who else might have lied?*

The ambassador flicked his fingers as if trying to rid himself of something foul. "He approached Sayer Goddard to offer the lands in exchange for money. Sayer did not need to pay. He had the blood oath. Regis is lucky that he wasn't skewered for suggesting a Scree would prefer to be given something he would earn by battle."

Regis had fooled her more than she thought. How could she have trusted him, let alone liked him? "It seems I am in your debt."

The ambassador laughed again. "You will not be in a position to pay back any debts after the duel. But, should you be victorious, be assured that cancels any debts."

Madeline ignored the assumption that she wouldn't win the duel. "I don't plan to be killed, but when I survive the duel, is this feud over? Will I have to look over my shoulder for the rest of my life?"

The ambassador smiled. "You have my word. If you win, there will be no one to come forward for revenge."

Madeline didn't like the sound of that. "What does that mean? I don't want to have to… I don't know, kill a whole family."

Waving his hand to dismiss the idea, the ambassador said, "There is only one left of Meesela's family. Her cousins made the mistake of attacking you against my orders. Those you did not kill, I have ensured will not be in a position to act. All except for Teeso, the youngest, he will fight the duel. He will kill you or die."

"How young"

"It does not matter," the ambassador said. "He is old enough to fight a duel."

It was brutal, but Madeline reminded herself that the Scree lived a brutal life, by the sword. That life had no room for weaklings. It seemed to work for them, but to Madeline it seemed unsustainable. "When do we start?"

They followed the ambassador through the building to the back, where a courtyard had been set up as an arena.

"Stand to the side," the ambassador instructed. "There are formalities."

Madeline scanned the area. It was roughly square. The sides of the space were lined with silent Scree. Sand covered the floor, but Madeline could feel the hardness of stone not far beneath. The silent audience stared at the center of a chalk lined square. Madeline felt a sizzle of danger against her skin. The Scree used chalk in their magic. She turned to Springheart and whispered, "Is it safe?"

He closed his eyes for a moment. "There is no magic, but it is not safe. You are going into a duel."

She grinned. "No kidding."

Jode stood between her and the chalk outline. "Madeline, you are going into this handicapped. Without your magic, you cannot defend yourself fully." His voice was low enough to keep the words between them, but she wished he hadn't spoken them before she had to do battle.

Fighting against a surge of panic, she wondered where it came from. Madeline realized her barriers were weak. Was that the reason she was easily led to believe Regis? Was someone sliding behind her mental protections? The fight wasn't a big problem because Jode had trained her to fight in any circumstance, and she had killed before, as much as she hated it. Fear was understandable, panic not. Jode was right though, without her magic she would be unbalanced. She touched the different areas of her body where her knives were hidden. "We don't have a choice," she reminded him. "If I don't do this, at least one Scree will continue to hunt us. We can't live like that. We can't raise a family that way."

Springheart stepped toward Jode and placed a hand on his arm. "Do not rush to judge what will happen. There are three of us here who want to walk out alive."

Madeline kept her eyes on the Scree lining the wall. They hadn't moved in the minutes since she'd stepped into the courtyard. A quiet noise behind her pulled Madeline's attention from the chalk square. The ambassador stood in the hall with a young man beside him. The Scree youth looked back at her seeming to summon every ounce of arrogance from the room into his gaze. He was only just out of his teens. Madeline relaxed a tiny bit, realizing she could fight him. It wouldn't be easy, but he wasn't a seasoned warrior, and that made a difference in a fight.

The ambassador gestured them to the center of the square. "We must complete the correct rituals before the duel can start."

"Rituals?" Madeline asked as she stepped to the center, hands itching to slip her knives out of their sheaths. The last ritual she'd taken part in was to rescue Lee from the Choi. Another death she hadn't meant to cause.

The ambassador spread his hands to encompass the entire party. "I announce this duel as the end of the blood feud between Meesela's family and the woman from another world. There are four members of her family still living at this moment. All were warriors. Three of the cousins have been sent to teach young Scree the art of the warrior. Something that they can do without their left hands. With their oath to the teachers, they renounce all claim to revenge. Teeso has chosen duel.

"Lady Madeline, you have some decisions to make," the ambassador said. Putting his arm around the young Scree, he continued, "This is Teeso. He has agreed that it is his duty to follow the code of blood."

The youth paled as the ambassador spoke. "I am bound to this action." He managed to say the words without stuttering.

"Now," the ambassador said, turning to Madeline. "You must make your decisions."

"What decisions?"

The ambassador moved Teeso to the other side of the chalk square before speaking. "You must decide whether you will fight, or you will put forth a champion. And you must decide on what you will cede to Teeso if he is the victor. Teeso had already agreed to provide you with the contents of his family treasury if you are victorious."

"What kind of duel are we talking about?" Madeline asked as she wondered what she could offer to him if she lost, not that she was planning to lose.

"It may be magic, or it may be physical," the ambassador said. "Does that make any difference?"

Madeline shook her head, knowing it would be fatal to admit weakness in anything. She turned to Jode and Springheart. Dropping her voice to a whisper, she asked, "Do you have any advice?"

"Allow me to be your champion," Springheart said before adding quietly, "I can fight with both magic and sword."

Madeline shook her head again. Unless something changed, this was her fight. "I am not sure that is a good idea. But it might help if you can tell if the boy has any power?" Madeline glanced at the youngster as she asked.

Springheart closed his eyes for a second then blinked them open. "There is magic in the room, but I cannot tell if this Teeso is in possession of it. It may be a spell to contain the effects of any magic used in the duel."

Jode touched her cheek. "I do not like this, Madeline. I should be your champion. It is my fault you are in this position. If had done a better job of protecting our party, this Meesela would not have died."

"And then Arabela would be facing another generation of that feud." The only value of the woman's death was to end a long feud between the two families. "And if they choose a magic duel? What then?" Madeline asked. "I will not put your life in danger. We are here because I killed that woman and her babies. I did that to save you. I am not going to throw that away."

He looked at the crowd and then turned back to say, "I do not wish to allow you to throw your life away. But I fear one of us will have to sacrifice. Do not lose, my love."

She smiled at him, knowing how much he wanted to take the danger from her. "I plan to do everything I need to do to avoid dying. But we must decide what I'll cede if we do not win." She touched her knives as she spoke, their presence adding a sharp comfort. "They don't know my magic is broken. If we pretend I still have my power that might be enough to push the decision to a physical battle."

Jode took her arm and drew her close. "Cede the Lower Plains. You will not lose, but with such a prize on the table it might cause the boy to make mistakes in his greed for our lands."

Madeline nodded at Jode. "How are we going to fake my power?"

"I can make it seem as though you shine with power by channeling my own through you," Springheart said, closing his eyes again. "I sense someone testing us, shall I reflect the probe?"

"Yes," Madeline said. Taking a deep breath, she turned to tell the ambassador her decision. "I will stand to fight. I place the Lower Plains as a prize."

The Scree standing witness murmured. She could almost hear the words, 'a woman is no challenge'. *Good, let all of them underestimate her.*

The ambassador spun to snarl at the crowd. "She has proven herself a worthy fighter more than once. The duel is valid." He turned to face Madeline again, his demeanor calm and civilized. "We will draw the stones. Enter the arena."

Madeline let go of Jode's hand and stepped to the center. Teeso obeyed the ambassador's gesture and joined her.

13

"Now," the ambassador said, drawing a small square box from his pocket. "I have placed three stones in this box. Teeso will withdraw one stone. Madeline, you will draw one stone. If the stones match, Madeline will decide the type of duel. If they do not match, Teeso will decide."

Madeline tried to access her magic again with no success. It just wasn't there. She would have to rely on luck and skill. She watched Teeso's eyes as he slid his hand into the slot in the side of the box. He stared at her as though to intimidate. It simply came across as petulance. He withdrew his hand and opened his fist. A pale blue oval glowed in his palm. He tilted his chin toward the box. "Your turn, human."

Madeline took another deep breath and reached into the box, keeping her own stare on Teeso's face. She felt two stones, one rough, and the other carved, neither oval. She tried to feel anything rising from the stones, something that would help her decide, but nothing happened. She drew them both together and rolled them in her fingertips for a second. Then she said a prayer, closed her hand around one, and withdrew it. Taking her eyes off Teeso for a second, Madeline turned to the ambassador. He nodded and she turned her hand over. Looking Teeso directly in his eyes, she opened her hand. His face tightened for a second before he regained control. She looked at the stone in her hand, red, with milky veins. It would be Teeso's decision.

The ambassador collected the stones and returned them to the box. He handed it to one of the waiting Scree and turned back to the two combatants. "When I leave the arena, Teeso will declare his choice of weapons and the duel will start. There are no rules except for these two; you must not use magic if the duel is physical, and you fight to the death."

He waited until they both nodded and then strode to stand beside Jode and Springheart.

Standing in the chalked arena facing Teeso, Madeline calmed her mind. If the boy chose magic, she was going to have to find a way to defend and misdirect. In the seconds it took her to achieve peace, she saw emotions flash across the Scree's face that might be fear in another being. She turned her attention inside her own body. The power was there, but something was holding it back. As she reached for it, the power slid away just far enough to be out of her grasp. It reminded her of the games of keep away the taller kids played against her as a child. The only way to deal with it then was to stop playing. She turned her focus back to Teeso. He was looking at his palm as if the stone still rested there.

Madeline bounced on the balls of her feet to test the depth of the sand. She didn't feel the hardness under her soles that had been there at the edge of the room. The boy was still staring at his hand. "How old are you?" she asked, feeling sorry for him. If he couldn't make this simple decision, he might be easy to defeat. *That isn't a comfort.*

He glared at her. "It does not matter. I am Scree and I will be victorious."

She gave a shrug. "My teacher would say nothing is certain. You need to make a decision. You can decide to let this go, you know. We can agree to simply walk away."

Muttering rose from the crowd and Teeso closed his fist. "Physical."

As soon as the words left his lips, he reached for his weapon, but Madeline was already flicking the first knife at him. He swore and twisted to the side. The blade fell to the sand and buried itself halfway to the haft.

Then he raced toward her with his short blade extended.

The hissing of the crowd faded as she focused on the next move, the next slash of her blade, the next twist to avoid Teeso's.

Madeline spun to the side just as he reached her. As she turned, she sliced at him with another knife. She felt her blade make contact, and then heard a hiss of pain from Teeso.

As she completed the full circle to face the next attack, dizziness overwhelmed her. She staggered, and then fell to her knees.

The world stopped spinning abruptly and she looked up to see Teeso standing over her, grinning as he raised his sword to impale her.

She kicked up and out, hearing a snap as his knee gave way. His sword arm bent and the blade skidded and dug into the sand as he keeled over.

Rolling onto her side, Madeline pushed herself into a crouch. She drew another blade and prepared to end the boy's life. A flash of memory drew her focus – Madeline, a knife in each hand sinking them into a woman.

Dizziness threatened her again, but she ignored it to narrow her focus on the boy struggling to rise and protect himself. His inexperience showing itself in the slowness of his movements. There was no other way for this to end. She could be merciful and kill him fast, but she had to kill him.

Teeso had managed to regain his feet, favoring his right leg, but standing. His sword in his hand, he tried to lurch toward her. She shot to her feet, knowing that she had to stay out of his reach. No matter how injured he was, he had height and weight on her, and that blade could still end her life.

Pulling her last knife, Madeline flipped it into throwing position. She raised her left hand to launch the blade at him.

Teeso grimaced in pain and reached to a sheath in the side of his leggings. Throwing knife in his right hand and sword in his left, he tried to stabilize himself.

The crowd started to shout encouragement and orders to the boy, but he seemed oblivious of anything outside of Madeline. He narrowed his eyes and swung his arm back to throw.

As he released the blade, his knee failed and the weapon went wide.

Madeline heard a gasp behind her and the crowd went silent. She turned, knowing that it made her vulnerable to Teeso's blade if he rushed, but she couldn't stop herself. Springheart was holding his arm, blood running through his fingers. "No, go back to the fight," he shouted.

Spinning back to face Teeso, Madeline dropped to her knees as his blade sliced through her shirt. She felt the burn of a scrape on her arm and the heat of blood running. *A scratch.*

She swiped at Teeso as he rushed her again, missing but deflecting his blade. His knee buckled again as he passed her.

Madeline knew she couldn't afford to waste a knife. Teeso was learning the difference between sparring and real fighting fast. She couldn't count on him making any more rookie mistakes. The damage was no longer slowing him down and the only way to win was to even the weapons so he couldn't take advantage of the longer reach of the sword.

She rose and took a step toward him. He was pushing himself up, still favoring the injured knee but it wasn't slowing him down enough. She rushed him swiping with her knives before he could regain his footing completely.

He focused on dodging her weapons while trying to raise his sword fast enough to stab. As she passed, Madeline leaned away from the blade and kicked at his knee again. The joint bent with a crack and Teeso screamed out his pain.

165

Madeline turned and released her throwing knives. One missed, skittering across the ground, the other sank up to the haft in Teeso's chest. He dropped his sword and grabbed the haft, pulling it out. The boy stared at the gout of blood that followed the blade, surprise flooding his face.

In what seemed like slow motion, Madeline watched Teeso collapse on the ground, blood soaking the sand.

The vertigo returned as soon as the boy hit the ground. Madeline lowered herself to sit, keeping her eyes on Teeso, unable to believe it was over.

The crowd started howling, the noise beating against Madeline, increasing the dizziness. She closed her eyes and ran the sand through her fingers trying to find her calm beach again, hoping it would stop the world spinning. She couldn't pass out in this crowd of maddened Scree.

A sudden shout silenced the crowd. The dizziness subsided enough for Madeline to feel safe opening her eyes. The ambassador was standing in front of her, his face tight.

"It is done," he said. "We will deliver your prize to the inn. Leave."

14

On the street, Madeline turned to Jode who was holding Springheart up. She was cold, the adrenaline from the fight making her tremble inside. She closed her eyes and then popped them open as the image of Teeso's blood soaking into the sand flashed into her mind. To avoid thinking about the duel, she asked Springheart, "How bad is it?"

Springheart smiled and said, "It is nothing, barely a scratch. Is your wound serious?" He was more pale than usual. A bead of sweat formed on his temple as she watched.

Madeline touched the wound on her arm, the blood already forming a scab. "Mine is really just a scratch," she said. "But you need Callisra. Can you walk that far?"

Jode shook his head before Springheart could answer. He lifted the elf and pointed his chin toward the inn. "I can carry him. We should go before he faints."

There were a few people on the street. Everyone they encountered glanced at Jode and Springheart before they hurried away. She was glad the inn was only a short distance. Her dizziness kept trying to come back, but she kept it at bay by focusing on the street ahead and willing it to recede.

She needed distraction. "Springheart, tell me about the quest."

When he didn't answer, she turned to look at him. He was even paler than before. His eyes were open, and he seemed to be trying to speak.

"No, don't worry. You can tell me after Callisra has healed you."

"It is fine, Madeline. I can tell you that you must find a way to unite the world. It is only together that we will be able to turn our world away from the gate between. The only way to stop a collision of worlds that will tear us apart."

Madeline stumbled when she heard the words. "How am I to do that?"

"Perhaps that discussion can happen when I am healed. I am sorry, but I have very little energy left." He closed his eyes.

The door to the inn came into view and Madeline felt relief wash over her. She couldn't just let Springheart's words lie there. He'd be healed in moments, and then they could talk it out. At least they could until one or both of them fell asleep from shock and loss of blood.

She led Jode into the lobby. It was empty. By this time, most of the other guests either were out for the night or tucked into their rooms.

"Take Springheart to our room, Jode." Madeline didn't wait for an acknowledgment. She knocked on Zerenia's door. No answer. She tried the door and it was unlocked.

Madeline slipped inside the darkened room, cautious of waking Zerenia if she was in. She reached for her power to create light and swore when it didn't respond. She pushed the door open to bring light from the lobby. When she turned back, she saw a body at her feet, Zerenia. Someone was slumped beside the open door to the room they'd locked Regis in.

The body at her feet groaned. Madeline bent to feel for Zerenia's pulse. The beat was strong so she moved to the second person. It was Simon. Blood caked on his temple; his face was ashen in contrast. She checked his carotid pulse, weak but still there.

"Simon," she said. He didn't respond. "Simon." She shook his shoulder, still no response.

Zerenia groaned again. Madeline turned away from Simon to see the woman rising. She hurried over to help. "What happened?"

"Callisra came to check that Regis did not need help." Zerenia lowered herself into a chair. "Simon came with her." She pressed her hand against her forehead. "I did not think that Regis had enough power, but he seems to have healed himself, at least enough to cause trouble. He took Callisra. We tried to stop him but he is much more powerful than…I am sorry, Madeline. This should not have happened to you in my house."

"Let me get Jode," Madeline said. "We'll figure it out. We'll make everything right."

She heard Simon groan as she ran from the room.

When she returned with Jode and Springheart, Simon was already sitting in a chair. Zerenia had managed to light enough candles to brighten the room and was wiping the blood from Simon's face. Madeline saw chairs upended and several shards of china in the corner.

"How badly are you hurt?" Jode strode to Simon's side as he spoke.

"I'll be fine," Simon whispered then cleared his throat. "We need to find them. He has Callisra."

Jode turned to Zerenia. "Do you have a healer you can call? Springheart is injured and we need every advantage."

"I can send a maid," she said. "But I have some herbs that will help." She left on her errands.

Springheart limped over to the chair and leaned on the back. "Tell me what happened, exactly."

Simon closed his eyes and began to speak. "We came to check on him. Callisra was concerned. She said I didn't need to come in. She said he was still sleeping and I could talk to Zerenia about music."

Zerenia returned as Simon gathered his thoughts.

"Here." She passed him a steaming mug and held one out for Springheart. "It will give you some energy until the healer comes."

Madeline smelled rosemary and thyme in the steam. The two men seemed to gain a healthier glow as soon as they consumed a little.

Springheart sipped again. "I thank you, Zerenia. This is a very potent brew." He nodded to Simon to drink. "Now, what happened next?"

"I heard a noise, like a scuffle, but quiet." Simon's voice was stronger. "I reached for the door, but they came out before I could open it. He pushed past me and Zerenia tried to stop them. He pushed her and she fell. Callisra tried to go to her, but he slapped her. I tried to stop him, but he stopped me. He reached out his hand and I fell. He didn't even touch me. I heard Callisra scream and he reached over and slashed my head with a broken saucer." He took a breath and sipped more of his tea.

"We'll find her," Madeline said. "We'll get her back. And we'll make sure Regis gets what he deserves."

Springheart placed his empty mug on the table. "Did he say anything?"

"No, at least not to me. I heard them talking in the room." Simon looked at Madeline then at Springheart. "Maybe he told her where they were going. Maybe you can do that spell. Like you did with the Choi. Recreate the scene?"

Madeline's heart broke. "My magic is unpredictable."

"I may be too weak," Springheart said. "But I know this spell. If we can do it, we will."

Madeline moved away and looked into the room. It was

undisturbed. A single bed and a small table were all the furnishings. She wondered if there was enough energy left of anything that had happened to fuel a spell. Then again, perhaps Regis had blocked any record.

"We can try," she said. "But we need to move fast. If we don't find out anything from the spell, where should we look?"

"He has few friends who would help him in this situation," Zerenia said. "He will be somewhere he controls."

Madeline looked around the small room where Regis had been captive. No clues jumped out at her. "Springheart, if we try it together, perhaps you can access my power."

Jode helped the elf to the room. Springheart looked up at her, "I don't know how successful we will be, but it is worth the try."

He pointed to the end of the bed. "Madeline, if you sit there, I can touch you without straining my injury. Jode, please leave us and close the door. It will take less power to fuel the spell if we contain the space."

Jode glanced at Madeline. She nodded. "I'll be fine. It won't take long."

When the door shut, Madeline turned to Springheart. "My magic is there, but it slips away as I try to use it. Maybe it will respond to you."

He took her hand. "I have done this before, but not in such a weakened state. If we wait for the healer, it may be better."

Madeline couldn't imagine sitting still for any length of time. "No, I can't sit waiting and doing nothing. If we are successful, then we have a head start. If we aren't, you can try again after you have been healed." She felt a twist in her stomach from the anger that rose suddenly. "I'm sorry. I... I am worried about my friend."

Springheart gave her hand a squeeze. "I understand. We will only know by trying. If you can settle your mind and let me see what I can do."

Madeline sighed and tried to push out the tension with the air. The fear flooding through her veins was not going to help find Callisra. She closed her eyes and visualized her beach, the warmth of the sand beneath her feet, the rush of waves against the beach. Her fear, dampened a little by every layer of the scene, was manageable by the time she tasted the tang of salt in the air. "Ready," she murmured, unwilling to chase the calm away by speaking loudly.

Springheart took her other hand. She felt his power slide in through her fingertips. At first, she felt her barriers start to rise, but she was able to exert control and hold them down. Hope rose in her that her magic wasn't irretrievable. The touch of Springheart's power was delicate and hesitant. Even without her own power, she could read how weakened he was through the contact.

He whispered, "I see what you mean about your power. It is as though you have given it to someone."

"I haven't—" He squeezed her fingers and she stopped speaking.

"Good, there is the spell we need." His tendril of power slid around her body. It was as though she'd swallowed a hot liquid and could feel it travel to her stomach. A tingle flooded her body making her gasp.

"Open your eyes," Springheart said.

Madeline looked and noticed she was sitting in the middle of a vision of Regis' legs. Springheart sat in the middle of Callisra. "Is he asleep?"

Springheart nodded. "Callisra is monitoring his health. See how she is touching his cheek?"

"Is this the last time they were here?" Madeline hated the fact that she could only watch the vision, not know the information about it.

"I think so, but I cannot be sure. Is there anything that gives you a clue? Callisra's dress? Regis' color?"

Madeline stared at the visions, trying to bring the details into focus. The harder she tried, the fainter the vision got. "Can you hold them stable?" She looked at Springheart and tried to jerk her hands away. He was almost gray; he was so drained. He held onto her hands despite his state.

"I will be fine. Remember a healer is coming," he said.

Fighting the urge to break the spell anyway, Madeline turned back to Callisra. She was dressed as Madeline had last seen her, but that didn't prove anything, she may have changed her clothes after they left, or she may not have. She turned her attention back to the bed. Regis opened his eyes.

Then the image flickered twice and disappeared.

"I am sorry, Madeline. I cannot hold it any longer," Springheart said, his voice faint.

Madeline shook her head. "Don't apologize. You did better than I could. We should go back to the others."

The healer had arrived while they were in the room. A tall man, a Mariai, his cheek scars white against his dark skin. He was talking quietly with Jode and, a much-improved, Simon. Zerenia was pouring tea for everyone and she raised a mug in a question as Madeline helped Springheart from the room.

"Thanks," Madeline said, taking the mug. "I need that. Springheart, go to the healer. We need to get moving as soon as we can."

The elf smiled at her and gave a graceful bow. Or at least tried, it became more of a faint than a bow. "As you command."

Madeline laughed, "Go get healed. I don't want to lose you now that I know you are a friend."

He stumbled toward the chair and sat. The healer reached for Springheart's temples and tutted as soon as he made contact. His voice was deep and comforting. "You have lost a lot of blood, elf."

Jode joined Madeline with Simon in tow. Kissing her cheek, Jode said, "You look tired."

She leaned against him, feeling comfort in his strength. "I'm not too bad. Do you have any ideas about how to track Regis?"

"There's a blood trail," Simon said. "Ulu, the healer, said it was human male. We figured we could follow the trail." He looked back to where Ulu was bent over Springheart. "As soon as he's finished healing our new friend we can go."

"Springheart won't be able to join us," Madeline said. "I don't need magic to see he's holding on by a thread. He'll sleep for hours when they are done."

"I can follow the blood," Jode said. "Zerenia says they had been gone less than an hour when we returned. She thinks Regis placed a spell on them to deepen their sleep. Do you need anything before we leave?"

Madeline felt for her knives. "No. I have my knives and Regis' magic will be weak if he used it to heal himself. Give me a minute to see how Springheart is doing and we'll go."

Ten minutes later Ulu had spared Madeline a bit of his energy and they were following the blood trail. "He is still bleeding, but Callisra healed him earlier," Simon said as they followed a trail of scattered drops.

"She must have gotten a weapon." Madeline kept her eyes on the street. "Of course she would have put up a fight when he took her."

They reached the corner and stopped. "Check the streets," Jode said. "The blood is running slower. It will not be as easy to follow."

Madeline watched as Simon and Jode scoured the streets for a red drop to lead them. She looked around to see if there was anything familiar down the cross streets, wishing she'd made sure they knew where he lived so they could eliminate the obvious.

The streets were silent. It was late and the bars were closed hours ago. Everyone would be deep into their sleep. Madeline raised her eyes from the street and a wet patch on the wall caught her attention. "He went this way," she called. "Away from the docks. I don't think we've been in this area before."

Three minutes and four blocks later, Madeline became suspicious. "Jode, stop for a second." She saw Simon start to protest and continued, "There is something wrong. Every time we think we've lost the trail, a drop of blood shows us the way. I don't think we are tracking him. I think we are following a trail laid for us."

"We still have to follow it," Simon said. "I can't just let him have her."

Jode reached for his knives. "Madeline means we need to be on guard. We are being led to a trap and we don't know when it will spring."

"Did you bring a weapon?" Madeline asked, drawing her knives from their sheaths.

Simon smiled and slid a short blade from inside his jacket, and a set of throwing stars from his pocket. "I would like to get in close and make sure he knows that he crossed the wrong man, but I'm happy to kill him from a distance. Let me have him."

Madeline had never seen this side of Simon and wasn't sure whether to be happy he loved Callisra this much, or sad that her friend was capable of this.

"Simon, killing someone changes you. I would not wish that on my worst enemy. Don't act without thinking. I want to know why he did this," she said.

He nodded. "I promise." He started to follow the latest marker, a smear of blood on a doorstep.

They followed the trail until they came to a street lined with darkened shops, the only light shining through a single window at the point where the street ended and the wall started.

"It seems the trail was to bring us here. Injured or healed, he will not have climbed the wall," Jode said. "We will approach from the center of the street. It will give us more room to maneuver."

"That's a good plan, but from the middle of the street, we can't see what's going on. Someone should go and peek in the window." Madeline pointed to a doorway across from the light. "That's deep enough for two of us to hide in while someone sneaks up and looks in the window. We can decide whether the middle of the street is safer after we know what's inside."

Jode followed her gesture. He nodded and said, "It will be dangerous for the person at the window. I think Regis is waiting for us and, no matter how we approach, he will strike."

15

"*I*'m not going to stand here waiting for you to decide on a plan," Simon said as he strode toward the light. "If he's waiting for us, then let's get it over with."

Madeline swore under her breath and hurried after Simon. He was going to get himself, and possibly everyone else, killed. Jode ran to get ahead of her, his free hand indicating that she should stay behind.

As they approached the door to the house, Madeline could see it was standing ajar. "Simon, let Jode go first," she called. "He's —"

"I know," Simon interrupted. "He's a trained knight." He turned and grabbed Jode's arm. "Okay, get in there. The longer we stall the more danger Callisra is in."

Jode entered. Madeline slipped quickly behind her husband, forcing Simon to bring up the rear. A position that prevented him from barging in and making things worse, if that were possible. A short corridor led them to the open doorway of the lighted room. Jode stepped aside to protect their backs as the other two entered.

Madeline saw a sparsely furnished room with four candles on a mantle. The hearth was filled with old ashes, the odor tickling her nose. A single wooden chair held Regis. A scan of the room showed Callisra bound and gagged in the far corner.

Regis was holding a blade in one hand, a trickle of blood flowing from a shallow cut on his wrist. His other hand held his ribs. Madeline touched her knives in reflex before she realized his wounds were more serious than he showed.

He coughed and grimaced. "Welcome to my home. Simple, yes, but I hope you will come to like it as I do."

"Let her go, Regis," Simon said, running to Callisra's side. "If you don't hurt her, I promise I'll be merciful."

"How kind of you," Regis mocked. "I admit I am at a disadvantage. Your wife does not restrict herself to healing, as you can see." He pressed a cloth against the wound on his wrist. "It did come in handy to lead you here. I did not have enough baubles on me to set the trail otherwise."

Simon lunged toward Regis, but Madeline grasped his arm as he passed. A sudden twist of nausea attacked her, dizziness washed over her and then faded. She felt Simon almost vibrate with hatred. Stepping closer and squeezing his arm, she said, "No don't do anything to him. At least not yet. I killed a boy tonight; I would prefer we don't kill anyone else if we can avoid it. I had no choice but to kill Teeso. We may have a choice here." As she spoke, she felt the echo of those deaths roll through her mind; Sayer taking his son with him, Meesela, Ophian, the Scree and now Regis. *Too much death.*

Shaking off her hand, Simon looked toward Callisra. Turning his gaze back to Regis, Simon said, "I know you aren't suggesting we let him get away with this. What options do you imagine we have?"

Madeline waited to see if Regis would offer anything, but he just smiled. She shrugged. "We won't know until we talk."

Simon stared at her and she saw his emotions range from anger to disbelief before he dropped his eyes and said, "What? What could he possibly say that would excuse his behavior? He kidnapped Callisra. He attacked Arabela." He flicked a glance at Regis who was still smiling but kept his eye on Jode who stood ready with a blade. "For all we know he's still attacking the Summer Lands. Until we get onto the other side of that mountain range, we won't be able to check."

A flush of magic burned Madeline's skin. Perhaps the mountains were blocking her magic and that's why it kept slipping away. She pushed aside the surge of hope; they could follow that idea later. "We won't know until we talk," she said again. "I am interested to know why Regis did this. It takes a lot to try to destroy your family, I don't care who you are. What is behind this, Regis? This is more than just being overlooked by a father who didn't know you existed. It has to be."

He leaned forward, pressing the cloth to his wound again. Madeline saw the red stain spread across the cloth. "Why can it not be that simple? You have no idea what my life was like." He flicked his collar straight with his free hand and smiled. "I suspect you had a wonderful family. Just like Alric, just like Tadric."

Madeline saw real hurt behind his casual tone. "There is no such thing as a perfect family." Madeline thought about the arguments she'd had with her father when she became a teenager, and how close they had come to breaking the family apart. "But why would your mother keep you secret from Maltius?"

Fire flashed through Regis' eyes. "Do not try to make this her fault. She loved me. Not like Maltius. He just abandoned her." He struggled to rise.

Jode stepped forward and pressed Regis back into the chair. "Maltius would not have abandoned a woman who carried his child. He wanted an heir. He would have—"

"He didn't, that is all that counts," Regis shouted before sucking in a sharp breath and clutching his chest.

Simon continued to glare at Regis as though he could pull information from him by sheer will. Madeline trusted Jode to keep Simon from doing something foolish and ran to untie Callisra. "Are you okay?" she whispered. "Did he hurt you?"

Callisra rubbed the circulation back into her hands. "I am not seriously hurt. But I should stop his bleeding, or he will be too weak to answer your questions."

Looking at Regis, Madeline saw the effect of the earlier battle and his new injury. "Will you let Callisra heal you?"

Simon hurried to his wife's side. "No. I will not agree to that. She needs all of her energy. He is going to die anyway, right?"

The lines around Regis' eyes deepened as Simon spoke. The strain was weakening him, despite his air of carelessness.

Callisra squeezed Simon's arm. "I know you are angry, Simon, but you do not decide who I heal. I cannot sit by and watch his pain. Pain that I caused." She waited for Regis to nod and moved closer. "I would appreciate it if you could hold his arms, Jode. I may not want him to bleed to death, but I do not trust him completely."

Jode and Simon restrained Regis while Callisra placed her hand on his wound. Madeline watched the familiar warm glow flow over the cut and disperse. When it was gone, so was the wound. Callisra sat back on her heels and sighed. "He is still weak, but now he will be able to answer your questions without further harm. He will need more healing soon, but I will not have the strength."

"Why did you do this? The kidnapping?" Madeline wished there was another chair in the room. Her head was pounding. She didn't want to show weakness in front of Regis by sitting on the floor.

He slumped. "I did not wish to die in the back room of an inn. I was conceived in one and I have always hoped I would die in a more… comfortable place."

Madeline felt the room shift and realized she was swaying on her feet. Callisra reached for her. "You must be exhausted. Let me help."

Waving her off, Madeline said, "I'm just tired." She hoped she wasn't lying to Callisra, or to herself. If she was lucky, she would be in bed soon. If she was really lucky, her sleep would not be haunted by the deaths of two people tonight.

She turned to Regis. "So, you expect to die? Is that what you think we came here for?"

"It is what I would do in the same circumstances. After all, if I am dead, I am no longer a threat. Simon looks as though he would kill me without thinking." A flash of anger crossed his face. "If Maltius had killed my mother before I was born, it would have saved everyone a lot of trouble."

"Are the attacks continuing?" Madeline snapped out the words. "Are you still throwing magic at the Summer Lands?"

Regis smirked. "Even my powers are not that strong. There have been no attacks for two days."

16

---

adeline touched her knives, suddenly tempted to end the attacks permanently and deal with the emotional draining later. A twist in her gut stopped her. "There must be a way to make this work without any more death."

"Unless you can give me back my childhood, I don't think so." Regis struggled to his feet. The wound was healed, but Madeline saw the effect of his blood loss. He would be an easy target if they wanted him dead.

He pointed to the chair. "I may be a bastard, but my mother taught me manners. Madeline, sit. You look like you are going to keel over. That would not go well for me, I think."

Jode took her arm. "He's right. You don't have to stand between him and the door. He is too weak to run."

She sank into the chair, wrapping her arms around herself to avoid touching the blood smeared on the arms. "I don't know what's wrong. I was fine a few minutes ago."

"You've fought a Scree today. You found out someone you thought was a friend had been betraying you," Jode said. "No wonder you are exhausted."

Madeline nodded and took a deep breath to try to clear her

head. The dizziness was trying to creep back, and she struggled to keep it at bay.

Regis turned to look at her. "You thought I was a friend?" he asked. "Why would you think that?"

Madeline looked up at him. He was leaning against the opposite wall. His face was twisted in a sneer, but she could see something different shining out of his eyes. It looked like hope.

"Yes," she said. "I thought you would be a friend. I don't know why. I've begun to think that you cast a spell on me. But, maybe, it's your powers that attracted me. I've never met anyone with more than one."

He laughed, hollow and bitter. "I inherited them. The charm magic came from my mother. The mind magic, from Maltius. Did you know he had mind magic?"

"He did," Jode answered. "Alric also inherited, perhaps Tadric will too."

Regis sneered again. "I suspect his power was useful when it came to seducing women."

Jode lunged at Regis. "He was an honorable man. Do not insinuate that he would have behaved in any other way."

"Don't, Jode." Madeline reached for her husband. "He didn't know Maltius. I'm sure if he had, things would be different. And he has a point. Maltius did break his wedding vows more than once. He couldn't have been that honorable."

Regis waved a hand in dismissal, not his usual elegant movement. "Be that as it may, I do not know where my ability to cast through mountains, or over oceans, comes from. My mother thought perhaps the magics combined."

"You can cast through mountains?" Madeline asked. Then feeling stupid for not putting it together earlier, she continued, "No don't answer that. Of course you can. You are attacking the Summer Lands." She rubbed her temples. "Can you still reach the Summer Lands?"

Regis shrugged. "I am weak from the injuries. I do not know how useful my connection would be."

The dizziness faded and Madeline's stomach stopped jumping. "How much information would you need to make contact with someone?"

"I cannot make contact with anyone. Your protective net is effective enough to keep my attacks from doing any damage." He laughed at the relief on her face. "Oh, eventually it would fail, but, for now, it is sufficient. And I suppose that it has done its job. My attacks will end with my death."

Madeline didn't like the resignation in his voice. "I can help with that. Will you be able to scry someone from my memory?"

He slid down the wall to sit on the floor. "Perhaps. I may not need your memory if you mean Lady Arabela. I know what she looks like. But it's academic. I don't have a glass to scry."

"Not Arabela, Blu. We need a shiny surface." Madeline looked at her companions, hoping one of them would pull out a mirror. She wasn't surprised when they all shook their heads.

Then Jode drew his sword. "Is this enough?"

Shaking her head, Madeline said, "Even if it was, would you let him hold the sword while we did the scrying?"

He shook his head.

"Let me take Callisra back to the inn. I can bring a mirror." Simon rose. "Five minutes."

Madeline nodded. "Something big enough to let both of us see what is happening. Like the size of a dinner plate at least."

Callisra protested, but Madeline assured her they would be okay without her healing power. "Get some rest. When we are done with this, I need you to figure out what is wrong with me and fix it."

While they waited, Madeline tried to steady her thoughts. She needed to determine how she would be able to get Regis in touch with Blu without opening the house to attack. Even with her magic, it would have been difficult to reach through the net.

"I know what you are thinking," Regis said. He had straightened his back against the wall and folded his legs into the lotus position. "You are thinking I will use the opportunity to attack. I assure you that I have not the strength to do so. But you won't believe me, will you?"

She shook her head slowly, sensing he had more to say.

He sighed. "I have a suggestion. I can bring you in easily. You will be able to see my magic. Have Sir Jode hold his sword to my throat. At your signal, he can end my life."

"How will she know you are not manipulating what she sees?" Jode asked.

"It is only for a short time. As soon as we contact Master Blu, he will control me."

Madeline wondered why she suddenly believed him. She joined Regis on the floor, facing him. "I think it will be all right, Jode. Regis, show me."

Regis reached for her hands. Madeline felt the invitation he sent her to join his power. She opened her defenses and was shocked to see colors swirling in her mind. Then the colors slowed and she saw them gather into three strands.

"Do you see it?" Regis' voice slid into her mind, stronger than his physical one.

Madeline said, "I see threads of carmine, sapphire, and emerald."

"That is my magic. Watch."

Madeline saw the carmine threads stretch then knot. As the knot tightened, Madeline heard a gasp from Jode and pulled her hands away. Seeing her husband rubbing his wrist and looking at the sword he'd dropped, she turned to Regis. "What did you do?"

"I am sorry, but I thought." He paused and his face became gray. After a deep breath, he continued, "I thought it best to show you a true demonstration. As you can see, it took most of my energy to do that."

She turned back to Jode and asked, "Are you hurt?"

He bent to pick up his sword. "Not permanently. He twisted the muscles in my arm, but only once. And now the pain is gone."

"I don't think he has enough energy left to swat a fly," Madeline said. "We will do this as soon as Simon returns, and then we will all go back to the inn."

Ten minutes later, Regis had a hand mirror balanced in his lap and Madeline sat facing him, her fingers on his knees. In the mirror, she saw the golden mesh that was protecting Arabela's house.

"How do we get through?" Regis asked, his voice a whisper.

Madeline visualized a delicate thread of power and Regis followed her lead with a line of sapphire thread. "Just place it on the surface and let me call Blu," she said.

In her mind, she saw the line make contact with the protections. Then her body warmed with power as Regis tied the other end to her.

"You are in control now," Regis said.

Seconds after she called his name, Blu send a ribbon of power to meet Regis' touch. "Madeline?" the monk asked.

"Yes, but don't open the protections." She explained the situation as concisely as she could. "And so here I am asking for your advice — again."

"You have done well. The attacks stopped two days ago. We hoped that you were the reason but have not let down our guard. Now what is the advice you would like? About your magic?"

"No." Madeline wished she could have said yes, but the situation with Regis needed to be resolved before he regained his strength. She could feel him feeding off her power a sip at a time. She sent him a command to stop and heard a chuckle for a response. She continued to speak to Blu, "What should we do about this situation with Tadric and Regis? My power can wait."

"Regis of the Downs," Blu said, more command in his voice than she had ever heard — or ever wanted to. "You are the child's uncle."

Madeline felt Regis tense.

"You have no doubt?" Regis asked.

"No. I feel Maltius in your power." Blu's voice was gentler. "You have a secret. Before we continue, you must tell us. If I am to help bring a resolution to this situation, I must know what you are hiding."

Regis did not respond.

"I can withdraw if you wish," Madeline said. "I do not need to know something you would prefer kept private. I will trust Blu's judgment."

Regis still did not respond.

Madeline kept hold of her curiosity. Pushing Regis would probably make him resist.

"I believed that Maltius rejected me," Regis said. "Everyone who knew him is telling me that is not true."

"The man I knew would not have abandoned a child and his mother," Blu said.

Regis let out a breath. Madeline risked losing the connection by opening her eyes. He was fighting tears. She tried to send reassurance through the connection, and when it didn't work, she gave his knee a squeeze.

"You are asking me to believe my mother lied," he said. "You are asking me to destroy any good memories I have, and replace them with nothing."

Madeline felt Regis' connection through the glass slip and she cried out as Blu's image faded and the sapphire thread flickered to sky blue, and then back to sapphire. If Regis was losing his power, they had little time. The connection flickered, and then Blu came back into focus as he took control.

"It is not necessary that your mother lied. Life is not a balance of truth and lie," Blu said. "Your mother may have believed what she told you."

Regis stiffened. "She did. I find it strange that her view of Maltius is so different from everyone else's." His voice was

187

fading and his breath was becoming labored. The power to maintain the scrying was too high for him to last much longer.

Madeline tried to give him more power, but she could not grasp it enough to push, and he was suddenly careful about how much he took. "Is it possible for us to move forward and leave the discussion of the past to a time when we are all stronger?" she asked.

"That is a question only Regis of the Downs can answer," Blu said.

Regis sighed and Madeline saw the lines on his face relax. "Yes, I think it is possible. And I thank you for thinking there will be a future."

Madeline gave his knee a squeeze. "So, what kind of future can we create? Is there any way Regis can make up for his behavior?"

Blu looked over his shoulder before answering. "I think it may be possible since no one has died. But it is not our decision. Lady Arabela must decide."

"Is she a woman to easily forgive?" Regis asked.

Madeline laughed at the idea of Arabela forgiving at all. The woman was her friend, but she could be so focused on the end goal, that compromise often didn't get near her line of sight. "I think it might be better if we presented her with a plan rather than just asked for forgiveness."

"I agree," Blu said. "You have something in mind, I assume."

Madeline noticed Regis' eyes close. She squeezed his knee hard. His eyes flew open. "Regis, take more power from me. We need you awake for a few more minutes."

"I cannot take more power without doing damage. I will be fine as long as I get rest soon, although your husband may have to carry me back to the inn."

Turning her attention back to Blu, Madeline continued, "I think the only way for this to work is for Regis to be part of the

Summer Lands family. Is there any way we can sell Arabela on trusting him?"

Blu smiled. "Regis, you have wanted a family for all this time. Would you be willing to join this one?"

"I will not be the poor relation living off begrudged charity." His words belied the hope she saw shining in his eyes.

"I am not proposing that," Blu said. "Lady Arabela is not one to provide charity. But she needs help to raise Tadric to be a good ruler. The child needs a man to help him grow to manhood."

"Regency?" Regis whispered. "Are you serious, monk?"

Blu didn't respond. Madeline recognized the look. He was waiting for Regis to think through the implications, to find his own answer.

"Are you proposing the ancient vows?" Regis finally asked.

"Yes," Blu answered. "I think that is the only way for Lady Arabela to accept your help."

"It is not what I wanted," Regis said.

Madeline could feel the lie in his mind and see it in the way his magic tried to uncoil. "It is," she said. "You wanted a family, not the land."

"You are so sure of that," Regis said. "I acted to take the land. I even offered it to the Scree once."

"So we heard tonight," Madeline said. "But be honest with yourself, Regis. You want a family. You keep telling us that Maltius abandoned you."

Regis stared at Madeline and she felt his life slipping away. She squeezed his knee again.

Looking at the ceiling as if for guidance, he said, "If she is willing, I am."

Blu turned to say something over his shoulder. "Lady Arabela will be here in a few minutes. You are sure you will take the vows willingly?"

"Yes," Regis said.

"What are these vows?" Madeline felt the situation slipping

out of her understanding. She didn't want Regis dead, but she didn't want him chained to some ancient ritual either.

Regis answered her, "I swear to protect and support Tadric at the risk of my life. If I betray him, the vows will cause my death."

"I can see where Arabela would be satisfied," Madeline said. "Are you sure you wouldn't rather just go back to the Downs and find something that interests you?"

"No one would trust me to stay there. I wouldn't trust me to stay there."

Before Madeline could argue, Arabela entered the image in the glass. "It is good to see you, Madeline," Arabela said. "You have news?"

"Yes," Madeline said. "The attacks are finished. This is Regis of the Downs. I'll let him tell you the story."

As Regis struggled through the confession, Madeline watched Arabela's reaction. Her friend went from curiosity to blazing anger by the end.

"And you think you can simply say you are sorry?" Arabela snarled. "I do not care if you are Maltius' son. No one attacks my family and lives, just ask Sayer Goddard."

Regis sighed. "I told you, Madeline. She will not be willing to accept me. There is no option for me, you must let me die."

Madeline shook her head. "No, keep the power attached, damn it! Arabela listen to me. The killing needs to stop. If you take revenge, who knows where it will lead. There could be someone to avenge Regis. I had to kill a Scree boy tonight because I killed his cousin to save Jode. It has to stop."

"Are you proposing I keep him here?" Arabela asked, gesturing to the room behind her. "I don't have a jail, or the people to guard him."

Blu made a calming movement at Arabela. "Madeline, can you strengthen the connection? I will have Arabela and Regis connect mind to mind."

Madeline looked at Regis, he shook his head and said, "I have no more to give and cannot take any from you."

Glancing at Blu, she tried to make the words sound casual, "I am having trouble accessing my magic right now. Is there something else you can do?"

"How long have you known this?" Blu asked. "Why did you not tell me immediately?"

"It's not a problem. I couldn't reach you before this. The mountains would have stopped you helping anyway." She was babbling and couldn't stop. Now that Blu was so close, all she wanted was to have him tell her how to fix it. Tears welled and she swallowed before speaking again. "We have more important things to settle. I was going to tell you as soon as we fixed the problem with Regis." She felt a probe of his magic touch her, and then a puzzled look cross his face.

"You are correct. I cannot help you over this distance. We will resolve this, and then you must hurry back." He turned to Arabela. "Are you willing to hear a solution to this problem?"

Arabela nodded. "I am willing to listen. I cannot say more."

Madeline let hope push the tears aside. If Arabela could find a way to compromise, everything would be okay.

Blu settled back in his chair, a pose that Madeline recognized from her history lessons. "It is not unusual for ruling families to disagree about a regency. There are rites to ensure a peaceful conclusion to such conflicts."

Madeline watched as the realization flooded Arabela's face. Before her friend could argue, Madeline said, "Arabela, don't tell me you have everything under control. As your friend, I am telling you, you look exhausted. Even though the attacks have ended, you are a mother, for most women that is a full-time job."

"I don't care," Arabela snapped. "Blu is here, and you will come back and help."

"Of course, we will help, but we are not family," Madeline said. "Nothing is as good as family."

Regis coughed and Madeline heard a rasp in his breath as he tried to get control. "Lady Arabela, I am willing to be bound by the vows, but if you do not decide quickly, I am afraid the decision will be made for us by fate."

Arabela glared. "I will not accept this arrangement just to keep you from dying. There will be no peace if we share the regency."

Madeline tried to think of another argument as she kept her eyes on Regis. Trying to think how she would be convinced in the same position but knowing it would be impossible to forgive someone who threatened her child. "Arabela, no one is asking you to forgive Regis. You don't even have to trust him. You just need to trust the vows."

"You don't understand, Madeline." Arabela's voice was quiet. Madeline knew the tone well from her first weeks in Cartref. Arabela was not going to be easy to convince. "Tadric doesn't need Regis. Jode can give him all the teaching he needs to be a man."

"I know he will. And he still will. We are not abandoning you, Arabela. But Regis is family. That is different." Perhaps if she kept repeating it, Arabela would hear the words.

Madeline turned her gaze to Regis, part of her wondering how she had so easily put aside his actions to become his advocate. He was breathing shallowly. If they couldn't get agreement in the next few minutes, she would break the connection and get him back to the inn. They could restart the negotiations later. Her attention came back to Arabela and the tension on her friend's face was smoothing into something softer.

"You may be right about family. We will see. You are right about the vows. I will trust them," Arabela said. "Can they be taken now?"

Blu turned his focus back to the glass. "He does not have the strength to take them now. Heal him and bring him to the Summer Lands."

Madeline nodded. "We will leave as soon as we are rested. Thank you."

"You look like you need a week of sleep, too," Arabela said. "And, Madeline, do not trust Regis until he takes the vows."

Madeline nodded. "We have to go. He is barely conscious."

As the contact broke, Madeline's sight faded to gray. She felt herself falling back and struggled to hold onto consciousness.

"Madeline?" Jode's voice seemed to come from a long distance. "Madeline, what has he done to you?"

Closing her eyes, Madeline answered, "Nothing, I am just really tired. How is Regis?"

She felt Jode's arms lift her from the floor. His breath was warm in her ear as he whispered, "He seems to be asleep. When the light left the mirror, he lost consciousness. I do not like that you also collapsed."

Jode placed her in the chair and the world stopped spinning. She opened her eyes and her equilibrium remained. Hope that she hadn't lied about the cause warmed her. "He is only just hanging on to life. I think he was feeding me power rather than taking it. We need to get home and have Callisra take care of us. Can you get us there quickly?"

"Simon, you take Madeline." Jode's voice was all business. "I'll follow with Regis. Have Callisra heal her as soon as you get in."

Simon bent to lift Madeline. "I don't know if Callisra has enough energy to heal both, but Ulu agreed to wait until we returned."

Madeline watched the others as Simon carried her from the room. Her vision faded again and she started to tremble from the cold. In the dimness, she saw Jode lifting Regis.

Jode whispered something in Regis' ear before he hefted him onto his shoulder. Regis must have woken because she heard him croak out, "Yes." Then darkness descended.

$\mathcal{M}$adeline opened her eyes as Simon stepped into the lobby of the inn. Callisra's hands were on her forehead even as they crossed to Zerenia's private room. A warm flow of energy came from the healer restoring Madeline to health. When Callisra was finished, Zerenia's maid passed a bowl of hearty soup to Madeline and placed a mug of tea on the table beside her.

She spooned the soup into her mouth as she watched Ulu strengthen Regis' body. She wondered if it would be so easy to heal his spirit. If Regis didn't want to live, no amount of healing would help. She prayed that her effort to restore the family would not be wasted. If he did want to live, would it be possible to give him enough strength to take the vows before they left The City?

"Madeline." Springheart's voice cut through her thoughts. "It is good to see you looking better."

"You too," she said. He was still pale, but it was an ivory cast to his skin now, not an ashen one. "Can we leave our talk until tomorrow? I'm not sure I am able to take in any more information tonight."

He smiled. "Yes, I was coming to tell you that I must go, but will return for breakfast. You should rest as much as possible." He bowed and left the room.

Madeline sipped the tea and waited until Regis was declared fit to talk.

Ulu raised his hands from Regis and excused himself, slipping out of the room before anyone could respond. Madeline looked around at their small group. Simon and Callisra were talking quietly in a corner, hands entwined. Jode was standing behind Regis' chair, looking ready to slice him in two if he so much as blinked wrong. Zerenia was doing the same thing as Madeline, sipping tea, and watching.

"Regis, we need to settle this," Madeline said. "Will you go and join Arabela? Take the vows and help raise your nephew?"

"I will," he said, sitting straighter in the chair. "I apologize for my depression earlier. It happens when I drain my power. I am grateful for the chance to have a family. As I am sure you are."

It seemed too easy to Madeline, but she would keep a close watch on him while they traveled back to the Summer Lands. "I found this little family when I came here. I didn't have one back where I came from."

He took a mug of tea from Zerenia and sipped. "Are you feeling well enough to hear what is blocking your magic?"

Madeline reached for her power, and felt it pull from her grasp. It was changing; now it was as though someone were tugging it away. "I am feeling better, but I think I have had enough to deal with tonight. Can it wait until morning?"

"Yes, it will wait." He smiled as though they shared a secret.

Curiosity drew the words out of her, "Perhaps you should tell me now. I can get all the bad news behind me and start fresh tomorrow."

"The children you bear are not bad news," Regis said.

The room went silent. Madeline looked around. She could tell people were speaking because their lips were moving. "I'm pregnant?" The sounds returned as the words came out. She looked at Jode; he was crossing the room, his guard on Regis forgotten.

"I thought you were aware? Hasn't Callisra checked your health?"

Callisra was still in conversation with Simon. They were not aware of anything going on outside their world. Zerenia leaned forward. "It would explain a lot of things. The vision could have been the babies seeking knowledge. There is often a gray space between conception and the spirits being settled on this side of the vision realm."

Jode engulfed her in his arms. "A baby, I had hoped, but..."

"No," Regis said. "Babies, there are two. You have a son and a daughter waiting to take over your lives." This was said loud enough to get the attention of the newlyweds. They hurried to join the conversation and congratulate Jode and Madeline.

Madeline pulled herself free of Jode's embrace. "My power? Could that be why I can't access it?"

"It is not usual," Callisra said and reached to touch Madeline's stomach. "I still do not feel them, but there is something odd. Regis, you might want to train as a healer."

He yawned. "I have no talent, or compassion, for that. We were tied very closely during the scrying. That is the only reason I became aware of the sparks of life. They are playing with your power, and I seem to be missing my far casting power. We can only hope that they are willing to relinquish these stolen magics when they are born."

Madeline frowned at Regis. His nonchalance was clearly a cover. "I am sorry, Regis."

He shrugged. "At least I have two powers left. It is you who is most at disadvantage. I do not know if they will give it back to you, but they will be powerful in their magic when they are born." He yawned again. "It will mean we cannot contact the monk or Arabela until we are through the mountains. Now I do not need to be a healer to know we should retire. Where would you like me locked up?"

Madeline looked to Zerenia who replied, "The same room you occupied before. Sir Jode can sleep outside the door if he wishes."

"I do," Jode said. "I think it is better to be overly cautious."

Madeline nodded. "I'll stay with you."

"No." Jode kissed her. His face still glowing with the news of the children. "You will sleep in our bed. A pregnant woman should not sleep on the floor if there is an alternative.

She didn't have the energy to argue. "Let's all get as much sleep as we can. Springheart will tell us what he needs tomorrow and then we can head back to Arabela's and start living a quiet life." *Well, I may have to save the world after that.*

THE NEXT MORNING, Madeline was the last one into the breakfast room. Everyone, including Regis and Springheart, was sitting around the largest table. To the other guests, they must look like a close-knit group of friends, or family. She hoped there was a chance that would come true. She filled a plate from the buffet and joined them. The thought of home prompted her to jump right into the topic. "Springheart, will you tell us the details of the quest now?"

"Good morning, my lady," he said. "I am ready to, but I would prefer that it is kept between the two of us."

Madeline looked around and nodded toward an empty table in the corner. "That's as private as we can get and still be in sight of Jode. I don't think he will let me out of his sight for a while."

"I have heard the good news," Springheart said as they moved to the other table.

Madeline put her hand on her stomach and smiled. "Yes, I don't even care about my power — much. Now, before you tell me this quest, you need to know that I do not keep secrets from my friends. This privacy is only temporary."

"I did not intend you to keep secrets, but there are some parts of the story I prefer to tell you in private. You are free to share as you feel appropriate."

Madeline leaned forward in her chair. "Go ahead."

Springheart pointed at her plate. "Eat, I do not wish to be responsible for your children going hungry."

Madeline picked up a pastry and waved at him to start.

"I am here because of a prophecy," Springheart said. "The elders of my tribe have received a dire message that the entire universe is in jeopardy. As I told you yesterday, you are the key to saving our world, and other worlds."

"Wonderful, another dire prophecy," Madeline said. She saw Springheart draw back. "No. I'm sorry. It's just that I came here to fulfill a prophecy and spent most of my time trying to figure out what I had to do. And it ended with the death of that Scree boy yesterday. At least I hope it ended. I thought it was over before."

"All actions have repercussions, do not blame yourself. This time it will not be difficult to know what to do. The prophecy was quite clear on that," Springheart said.

"That seems to be contrary to what I know about prophecy," Madeline said. "Isn't it usually all cloaked in mystery and confusion?"

Springheart laughed. "Yes, that is true. I am sorry to say that we do not know how you are expected to do this thing."

"Why did they send you?" Madeline knew she was stalling, but she wanted to finish her meal before she was dragged into something else she couldn't avoid. And since she was eating for three, breakfast might take a while.

"I have no family and could leave immediately," Springheart said.

"That can't be all of it. You said that there were things you didn't want to tell me in front of the others. I haven't heard anything like that."

"You are right," Springheart said. "Let me fill your plate again before I tell you my embarrassing secrets.

He rose before she could answer. Madeline smiled and watched as he chose a plateful of food for her as though he was solely responsible for her health.

When he placed the food beside her, he started talking, "The secret I hope you will keep from becoming public is a private shame." He raised an eyebrow.

"I won't make it public," Madeline said. "You don't have to tell me if it isn't about the prophecy."

"No, you must know this. I asked you to trust me without knowledge of who I am. This is my history."

She waited while he gathered his thoughts.

"Elves take family seriously. It is sacred to us. Our lineage is memorized and repeated on ceremonial days. My lineage is not known. I am fatherless. That is shameful to our people."

"What happened to your father?" Madeline hoped it wasn't Maltius as they had once suspected.

"My mother could not tell anyone. She was here in The City for a while. She left, taking a ship to the islands. When she returned home a year later, she was heavy with child. I came before she was able to tell her people who the father was. She died bringing me to the world."

"I am so sorry, Springheart." Madeline reached for him. "That must have been horrible for her."

He pressed his lips together. "I was raised by my grand-mother. She was kind. People were all kind."

"And no one tried to find your father?"

"There was an attempt, but there were no elves on the islands when the elders of my tribe sent messengers."

"And you know your father was an elf?"

"Yes, that is all we know. I am full elf," he said. Looking at her, he frowned. "You thought I was part human? Ah I see. You thought I was another of Maltius' offspring. No, he was a good friend to my mother when she lived here, but it was always a proper relationship."

Madeline took the last pastry, amazed that she had managed two full plates of breakfast. "I admit that's kind of a relief. All we needed was another claimant to the Summer Lands. I'll keep your secret. Now, what do I need to do for the prophecy?"

"You do not ask why? You do not wish proof of the prophecy?"

Springheart's question surprised Madeline. She had no doubt that the prophecy was true. She didn't know why, but she believed. "No, I trust that you believe it, but I would ask why me?"

His words came out in a rush. "I will answer your other questions first. We need you to come and read the signs to understand what actions you must take. We believe this must be accomplished within the next three months. And as to your babies, I do not believe you will endanger them by undertaking the quest. I believe that by avoiding your role, your babies will not live to be birthed because the collision of worlds will kill all life on Cartref, and the other worlds involved."

Madeline wished she had her magic. Wished she could reach Blu. Wished she knew what to do. She put aside her wishes and said, "This is no longer just between us. Jode, Simon, and Callisra must be told. I need their council. I need Jode to agree to this before I can accept the responsibility."

Springheart nodded. "I understand. I only ask that you send Regis back to his room. Until he has taken his vows, I do not fully trust him. When he is gone, I will explain to your companions."

18

By the time Regis was locked away, they had the breakfast room to themselves. Springheart had finished explaining the quest and now the four of them were silent.

After a few minutes Jode said, "I think there is nothing to discuss. We have no choice about the prophecy. We must follow it. We do have a choice about how we proceed."

"As long as we proceed quickly," Springheart said. "I believe we must leave for the Elven lands tomorrow, if not today."

Madeline felt her magic rush to burn her skin. She pushed her third plate of food away. "Today is too soon. Springheart, you and I are still recovering. It would not be useful for us to fall ill on the journey. I think we should go tomorrow. Simon and Callisra can escort Regis to the Summer Lands. Maybe you can do something that will ensure their safety, Springheart." She hated having to ask him to take care of things. Only a year with magic, and she was already dependent on it.

The elf raised an eyebrow. "I will scan his intentions. If he is sincere, there will be no need for anything else. If not, no magic will hold him. He can be shackled just like anyone. Is that sufficient?"

"Wait a minute," Simon said. "You can't just cut us out of this quest. You can't just rush off to save the world without us, without me."

Madeline's heart broke at his words. "Simon, you came here to this world by mistake. You have followed me into everything. You have to think of Callisra now. I need you to be safe."

"No." Simon struggled to find the words. "Your magic is gone. You need us. Anyone can escort Regis."

Callisra took his hands. "I agree. I'm sorry Madeline, Simon is right. I think we should stay together. We have always succeeded together; we should not change that."

Madeline looked at Jode, and then placed her hands on her belly. There should be nothing there yet, but she felt a connection. "I don't think I trust anyone to take Regis back."

Jode laid his hand atop hers. "You seemed to think he was sincere. Are you having second thoughts?"

"No. I just know that things can change. I don't want to come back from saving the universe to find Arabela, Tadric, and Blu dead."

Springheart narrowed his eyes. "I understand you have some prescience."

"Yes, but it usually comes with physical manifestations. I feel nothing of the usual heat on my skin now."

He inclined his head. "It may be that you have lost the warning, but not the talent. It seems we will bring Regis with us."

"I think that's best," she said. "I'll send a message to Blu. It should arrive before they start to worry."

Jode kissed her cheek. "I will make sure he is no danger to us while we travel."

Madeline sighed. Hoping that this would be her last adventure, she looked at the small group of people around her. Then she grinned at Simon. "It seems we are three people short of a full quest. Perhaps a few dwarves will knock at the door tomorrow." They both laughed at the puzzled looks on the faces of their companions.

WANT MORE?

A final prophecy demands a sacrifice from Madeline. Use the QR code to grab your copy of End of the Tunnel and find out if she can decode the clues in time.

Sneak peek next.

* * *

If you enjoyed reading A Twist of Power, please consider helping other readers to find the story by leaving a review.

CHAPTER 1

*J*t had been two months since her party had arrived in the elven homeland. A beautiful area of rolling hills and small lakes surrounded by giant willows, and something that looked like a magnolia, but had tiny flowers. The library was set in a small grove. Domed roofs of the clustered buildings dwarfed by the ancient trees. The rooms were filled with scrolls and books preserved by a spell that kept the air dry.

Madeline remembered feeling both awe and crashing disappointment when she first stepped foot in this room. Awe for the sheer age of the knowledge contained in the room, and disappointment because she wouldn't be able to read any of them. She'd learn to speak the common language, but reading was a whole other skill. Each race had its own script, and none of them made sense to her. Amberbirch had solved the problem. Taking a thin sheet of paper, and speaking a few words over it, she handed it to Madeline. "This will help you understand what is written. Place it on top of the page you wish to read, and it will become clear to you."

Since then, Madeline had been able to read the words, but

most had not become clear. They were running out of time to close the gate between worlds before the next battle started.

"Another dead end, Madeline?" Amberbirch asked as she entered the room. The elven woman was small. Elves are about two thirds of the size and mass of a human. They appeared ageless at first to Madeline. Dressed in a loose gown that was the same color as the deepest part of the lake, with her hair braided in a complicated pattern that reached her hips, Amberbirch gave the impression of being willowy, but without the height.

"Not exactly," she answered, rubbing her back to ease the stiffness from bending over the scroll for so long. "I think I may have found more details of the past invasions, but some of the writing is faded so much that I can barely read it."

Behind Amberbirch came a servant bearing food, caf, and wine. Jode joined them as the servant finished laying out the meal.

"I can have someone rewrite it," Amberbirch offered. "Elven eyes are sharper. It may help."

"I don't think we have time for a rewrite." Madeline looked at the piles of books in the room, knowing she didn't have time to read all of them once. The gate would open soon, and if she didn't find a way to seal it, everyone here would die in the battle. They would only be the first of thousands. "I'll take it outside tomorrow. The sun will help make the words more clear."

Amberbirch reached for Madeline's hand to help her rise, but she waved it away, reluctant to rely on others until she really was unwieldy with pregnancy. The small bump was getting to the point where she'd soon have to find a different posture. She had already had to give up riding, she was going to cling to the last shreds of independence as long as she could.

Jode touched her shoulder to pull her attention away from the pile of books. "You are tired. When did you last eat?"

Madeline pushed back from the table, loath to abandon her studies, but knowing she was getting tired and needed a break. "I guess I could do with a real meal. Perhaps I can come back to this later."

Jode took her arm and led her to the table, his assistance always welcome. "We will eat together. Tell me what you found, and we may be able to discover a truth between us that is hidden to you."

"Don't you get tired of talking about this?" Madeline longed for a time when she could sit alone with her husband and talk about anything, or nothing.

"It is not a subject we can avoid, so let us embrace it. If I am unable to help, it will be of value to have Amberbirch hear what you think you have learned. Perhaps you understand a different meaning because you come from a different world."

Madeline knew that it was certain that she had a different understanding. "It's probably why I get to be The Chosen One. My misunderstanding will uncover the secret."

Amberbirch poured caf for Madeline and wine for herself and Jode. "You are both right," she said. "Without discussion, you will never know if there is a difference between what you understand and what we do."

Taking a sandwich from Jode, Madeline gathered her thoughts and quelled an odd feeling that she should keep her information close. This was the same as when she did a case review with her colleagues at home – no, on earth – no, the other earth. Oh shit. "Let's start from the beginning," she said. "You know that there are supposed to be multiple universes."

Jode nodded and added, "When worlds come close enough, a gate opens allowing people to cross. But only warlike people seem to come here. It is odd that only the elves seem to know this."

Madeline looked at Amberbirch who was studying her glass of wine. If the elven woman had nothing to offer, then there was probably no difference yet to be discussed. "Yes, this is the first time that people outside the elven world have been brought in to help."

Amberbirch looked at them. "It has been the duty of the elves to save the world since time began. I will be happy to have you succeed, Madeline, but the army will come in case we have to do our duty."

"Some of the invaders survive," Madeline said ignoring the implied dig at her ability.

Smiling at them, Amberbirch straightened a fold in her robe. "The Tryll haven't yet integrated."

Not understanding why the woman was suddenly undermining them, Madeline responded, "If the elves kept this a secret, how did the others explain new types of people showing up?"

Amberbirch rose and bowed to Madeline. "I think we are both feeling the stress of our study. Perhaps, it would be better if Jode acted as your sounding board." Without waiting for either of them to respond, she gracefully exited the room.

Shocked at the change in Amberbirch, Madeline looked at Jode to see him frowning. The woman had never been anything but a gracious host. Although the library wasn't her home, she was there to mentor and guide Madeline as she searched for ways to fulfill the prophecy. "What just happened? Did I step over some line of etiquette?"

Jode still stared at the archway, apparently as surprised as Madeline at the reaction. He shook his head as if trying to bring himself back to the present. "Not one that I am aware of," he said. "Perhaps she took your words to mean that the elves should have asked for help. It is clear they are proud of their role as safe keepers."

"So much for getting help." Madeline placed her empty mug on the tray for the servants to clear later. "I have only found hints and clues that there is an answer. I think that we need to return to the gate."

"I do not like that place." Jode stood and walked to the

window. "I always feel that we are under attack when we are there."

They had been there only twice, but she knew the feeling he meant. A feeling of being watched, of evil waiting for a moment of indecision, or inattention. "We will have to go there, Jode." She joined him at the window and patted his hand, a gesture meant to reassure, but it didn't help quell the dread that had crept over her with his words. "I don't think we can hope that the answer is here. That we will just have to go to the circle with the solution."

"It is not just your life I worry about."

She turned to look at the table of books. "I know. It's everyone's life."

"I meant the children."

Feeling guilty that they hadn't been her first thought, Madeline turned back to Jode. "Yes, but if I don't fix this, they will die." The words hurt to say. The thought of her babies in danger chilled her body from the inside.

"It is not something I can think about," Jode said, joining her back at the books. "Shall I stay?"

She warmed at the thought of company. "If you find sitting watching me read interesting, I would love you to stay. It gets lonely in here."

He pulled a chair from the corner and sat beside her. "You can tell me what you are reading. We will discuss the meanings as you find them."

Madeline pulled the next book on the pile toward her, opening it to the first page. Placing her translation sheet on the title page she read aloud. *"The life of Timberraven, a scholar of the last invasion."*

Turning to next page, she slipped the translation sheet on top. The words blurred, something that happened in about half the books she read. Then the words came into focus in patches. It took a few minutes to get all of the words clear enough to read, the final ones flickering a few times before settling.

"I don't know if that means anything," she said when Jode asked if it was normal. "I'll ask Amberbirch, but not just now. I think she needs a bit of alone time."

"Let someone else smooth the way for you."

Madeline let the tension she was feeling out in a laugh. "I can be tactful," she said when she had her laughter under control.

"Yes, you can, but you don't have to do everything. Regis and Springheart can do more than just help you read documents."

Madeline agreed, not really believing she could delegate any of the important tasks. Whatever had twisted Amberbirch's panties was probably something simple. Having to help The Chosen One find a way to seal the gate, was probably almost as stressful as being The Chosen One. "Why don't you get them doing that? I'd rather she was back to her pleasant self tomorrow at the gate. Like you say, it feels like there's already an enemy waiting to attack there. We don't need to bring any animosity with us."

Jode kissed her and left with a promise to return and help. As soon as she was alone, Madeline put aside the book she'd been reading and started flipping through her notes. They were going to the circle of stones that formed the entrance to the gate between worlds. She didn't have any information on how to seal the gate, but there was a book that described the gate, and the construction. There had to be something useful in there, something to guide them tomorrow.

She found the notes and the book and had them laid out and was settling in when Amberbirch joined her. "I apologize for my behavior," she said from the archway. It felt as though she was waiting for permission to enter the room.

Madeline stepped away from the papers she'd spread out, knowing that if she sat at the table, her attention would wander to the information. She'd already done something to upset Amberbirch. She wasn't willing to chance doing it again.

"We are all tired and tense," Madeline said as she approached.

"Let's just forget about what happened." She took the woman's hand and drew her into the room. Telling Amberbirch about the planned trip in the morning, Madeline asked about the problem with the translation page.

Amberbirch frowned. "It should not happen. Please, show me."

Digging out *The Life of Timberraven*, Madeline repeated the exercise. The page became clear immediately. Annoyed, Madeline turned the page and said, "Let me try a fresh page."

The next page came clear immediately, as did the following five pages. "Great, it's not going to happen while you're here."

Amberbirch took the translation sheet from Madeline. Holding it up to the light coming through the window, she placed her hand on the page and muttered some words. "I have recharged the spell, but this fuzziness should not be happening at all. Let me know as soon as it does in the future."

Madeline nodded and hoped that it would happen soon.

CHAPTER 2

$\mathcal{T}$he evening came too soon for Madeline. No matter how many candles were lit, there was never enough light to bring out the faded words on the pages in front of her. She'd triggered many a headache trying to puzzle out the meanings of the texts.

She stretched and heard her bones crack from being held in one position too long. Regis and Springheart were huddled over other scrolls, making notes now and then. The frowns on their faces showed their lack of progress. "I think we need to find another way to do this research," she said. "We don't have time to read all these books and scrolls. And without an index or something, we'll just be feeling around in the dark."

The two looked up from their work. Springheart slight and blond, Regis not much bigger, but dark haired, they could have been brothers. At one time, she'd suspected they were, but now that she'd seen more elves, there was no doubt that Springheart was a full elf and Regis was all human.

"What do you have in mind?" Regis asked. "My magic is at your disposal if that will help."

Regis carried powerful magic. Even when she'd seen how

complicated it was to wield three types of magic, Madeline had been jealous of his talent. The babies growing inside her continued to hold her magic hostage. There was no guarantee that she would ever regain the power. It was a hole inside her. The power only flowed through her for a short time, but it had become so much a part of her that she didn't feel like herself without it.

"I wish I did have some idea," she admitted. "All I know is we aren't getting anywhere doing this. In my old world, we had a saying, repeating the same actions and expecting different results is the definition of madness."

Springheart chuckled. "Perhaps your idea of visiting the site where the gate will open again, is the best approach. Now that we have a little information, perhaps we will gain more knowledge from the writing there."

They had visited the site of prophecy shortly after arriving at the library. A circle of a hundred stones with words written on each of the massive pavers. The words drew the reader around in a circle to the center, like a simple labyrinth. The center was a deep hole, big enough for two people, but with no way to enter other than to jump to probable death.

"Jode doesn't like the idea, but I agree." She placed her hand on her belly. It was too soon for her to feel the babies moving. It felt like there was a presence there anyway. Something that acknowledged her touch. "Regis, could you try to contact Blu? I know they are on the road to us, but if Blu has some advice, it would be better to get it now."

"I'm sure Simon and Callisra are hurrying the journey, Madeline," Regis answered. "I will try, but without an idea of where they actually are, I don't hold much hope."

Simon and Callisra had taken a lot of convincing to go and get Blu to join the party. Madeline knew that the soonest they would arrive was in a week. "We won't know unless we try."

The two men rose and held out their hands to assist her in

gaining her feet. "You should not spend the entire day sitting," Springheart said. "Pregnant women need exercise."

Madeline gave a bitter laugh. "I know. I'll get all the exercise I need when we've figured out what to do." And tomorrow she'd be on horseback, probably for the last time until after the babies came. Walking around the circle of stones would be exercise enough for now.

Springheart and Madeline joined Jode and Amberbirch who were sitting around a fire pit watching as the sun dropped behind the grove of trees. When they were seated, Amberbirch instructed the servants to bring refreshments. She had taken on the role of hostess as well as being the person who advised them.

"What have you learned today?" she asked as wine and tea were poured. "Are we any closer to stopping the next invasion?"

Glad that Amberbirch's mood had improved, Madeline wanted desperately to say yes, but she admitted it had been another day of dead ends and obscure texts. "We'll go to the site at daybreak."

Amberbirch straightened and cast her glance to Springheart. "That is a long journey if you have learned nothing to help you."

It wasn't what she wanted to hear, but Madeline couldn't find any way to argue against it. While she struggled to find a way to lighten the pessimism, Jode put his arm around Madeline and drew her close. "I think a day away from the library will do our scholar some good. We can make a picnic of it for all of us. It is not that far."

"A picnic would be fun," Madeline agreed, thinking that the circle was the last place she would choose to relax and have fun. "I'll bring my notes, and maybe we can decipher some of those words."

Amberbirch was silent and Madeline watched her fingers whiten from the tightness of her grip. No one else seemed to notice the tension. Madeline wrote it off to the same fear they all had. That the knowledge they needed would stay hidden, and there would be a battle of monstrous proportions when the gate opened.

"I think you are probably right," Amberbirch finally said. "We can take a day to get fresh air and a new perspective. I am sure that will make all the difference."

Regis joined the group taking a glass of wine and lowering himself to a brightly embroidered cushion. "I regret I was not able to contact Blu. It seems we will have to wait until they arrive."

"Thanks for trying." Madeline placed her empty teacup on the floor. The wine was tempting, and she'd been assured that it wouldn't hurt the babies, but her conditioning was that pregnant women didn't drink, so she stuck to water, or tea.

Jode gave her a gentle squeeze of reassurance. "They will arrive in time. I have every confidence in Simon. And Arabela will be mustering an army to fight the battle if needed. It has been done before. It will be done again. This time the elves will have help."

"Each time the battle becomes worse, the casualties larger," Amberbirch said. There was a tone in her voice of regret, some pain Madeline couldn't name. "We need to close the gate and put an end to this cycle. We may not survive this battle. Even if we do, we will definitely not survive the next."

Wiggling out of Jode's embrace, Madeline placed her hand on Amberbirch's shoulder. "We will keep trying until the end. If that is a battle, then we will win and continue to search for a way to close the gate."

The woman looked at Madeline's hand then into her eyes. Madeline saw an echo of the pain she'd heard in the words. "Let us hope your optimism isn't misplaced."

Madeline smiled. She had faced, and overcome, so many chal-lenges since coming here that she would never have even imagined in her old world. "Optimism, or luck, it doesn't matter. We'll be successful."

* * *

A FINAL PROPHECY demands a sacrifice from Madeline. Use the QR code to grab your copy of End of the Tunnel and find out if she can decode the clues in time.

FREE EBOOK

Claim your copy of Obstacles of Magic when you use the QR code to sign up for my newsletter and learn more about Madeline's history with magic.

ALSO BY P A WILSON

For more books by P A Wilson

Use the QR code below or go to pawilson.ca

ABOUT THE AUTHOR

Perry Wilson is a Canadian author based in Vancouver, BC who has big ideas and an itch to tell stories. Having spent some time on university, a career, and life in general, she returned to writing in 2008 and hasn't looked back since (well, maybe a little, but only while parallel parking).

She is a member of the Vancouver Writers Social Group, The Royal City Literary Arts Society, and The Surrey Writing Workshop. Perry has self-published several novels. She writes the Madeline Journeys, a fantasy series about a high-powered lawyer who finds herself trapped in a magical world, the Quinn Larson Quests, which follows the adventures of a wizard named Quinn who must contend with volatile fae in the heart of Vancouver, and the Charity Deacon Investigations, a mystery thriller series about a private eye who tends to fall into serious trouble with her cases, and The Riverton Romances, a series based in a small town in Oregon, one of her favorite states. Her stand-alone novels are Breaking the Bonds, Closing the Circle, and The Dragon at The Edge of The Map.

For more information
www.pawilson.ca
pawilson@pawilson.ca

ACKNOWLEDGMENTS

People think that the process of writing is solitary. That's not the case for me. I have help from so many people it would be hard to acknowledge everyone, but I'll give it a try.

The support and inspiration I get from my writer's groups is incalculable. The Vancouver Writers Social Group opens my mind to other ways of telling a story. The Royal City Literary Arts Society gives me the opportunity to meet and share with other writers who have more knowledge than I do. The Other 11 Months group is where I learn about getting the words on the page. And my critique group who helps me find the best parts of the story I want to tell. Thanks to all of the members of these great groups.

Last of all, but definitely a huge part of the process, my beta readers. These are the people who love stories and are willing, and more than able, to tell me if my finished story is ready for you, my readers.